Tagger

Bearing Witness

ANTHONY S

Copyright © 2023 Anthony S
All rights reserved
First Edition

Fulton Books
Meadville, PA

Published by Fulton Books 2023

ISBN 979-8-88505-943-5 (paperback)
ISBN 979-8-88505-944-2 (digital)

Printed in the United States of America

Contents

Preface v
Acknowledgments vii

Chapter 1 1
Chapter 2 9
Chapter 3 17
Chapter 4 29
Chapter 5 41
Chapter 6 53
Chapter 7 63
Chapter 8 77
Chapter 9 89
Chapter 10 105
Chapter 11 119
Chapter 12 139

Preface

God said, "Go into the world and be disciples," letting others know that there is hope and know who He is; He didn't say exactly how to accomplish this; but surely, he wants us to reach as far as we can, using discernment to (embrace) gravitate the purpose of love and its meaning, salvation and its meaning, and the importance of both. I truly believe He means that if it's in alignment with His word, then have at it. As long as the seed is planted, He will harvest the seed that one plants. Jasper has acquired a sixth sense. After he encountered the love of Jesus personally, his pens, pencils, paintbrushes, or aerosol paint were anointed by the Master Himself. His unique art displayed throughout the city spoke to others in a way that was both breathtaking and meaningful. He captured their attention. "If a doctor is a doctor, then let him be the best doctor that he can be. If a singer is a singer, then let them be the best that they can be. If an architect is an architect, then let them be the best that they can be. If a street artist can be a street artist, then let him be the best that he can be. Along with the anointed sixth sense, carry on. This is what empowered him to seek lost souls. So be it! This is the story of Jasper carrying out his diligent plan of discipleship!

Acknowledgments

I want to first acknowledge our Heavenly Father for protecting, guiding, providing, and sustaining us. I also want to acknowledge my oldest brother, Cliff, who passed away. If it were not for our Heavenly Father, I don't know how I would have coped. I truly miss him.

I also want to acknowledge the innocent victims that were slaughtered/killed senselessly in our country and around the world. May they rest in peace. I want to honor those who have supported and encouraged me. I want to acknowledge my wife, Cheryl; my moms Dee Parker, Betty Comins, Sherrie Boyd, Millicent Lipkin, and Virginia Conwell; my children Toni, Marvin, and Charnell; my grandchildren Israel and Immanuel; my siblings Duffy, Yancy, and Rodney; my in-laws Felix and Silverstine Williams; my close friends Blaze, Mr. and Mrs. Brian Holt, Mr. and Mrs. Tim Moore, Pastor Jerrod and wife, Mr. and Mrs. James Baker, Pastor Sheppard and wife, Mr. and Mrs. Larry Yates, Mama Sherri and sister Mary Boyd, Brother OJ and wife, Mr. and Mrs. J. Lipkin, R. Palmer, Daryl Canty, Mr. and Mrs. Robert Nealey, Ruth Golden, Felicia Garrett, Zenetta Yarbrough, Rita and Randy Patrick, Mr. and Mrs. Kevin Terry, Kenny Creech, Kurt Montgomery, Mr. and Mrs. Ruben Martenez, Todd Frye, Lil sis (Squishi), Linda McMillian, Mr. and Mrs. Marlon Jones, Cory, I'll, Elliott, Woo, Bishop Jim, and Pam Baker; Mr. and Mrs. Bobby Griffin; my Peach Church Family; Steve Russo; first responders; Mz. Peachez; Sam Archer; Ryan Collins; Matt Massy; Belle Publishing; Angel Charmaine; LaRay Johnson; military veterans who served for our freedom; those who are sick; those who are lost in Christ; and those who have fallen from Christ!

Blessings to you all!

Chapter 1

Hard Times

Jasper was born in the housing projects in South Central Los Angeles to his parents, Jake and Dottie Smith. He is fourteen years old; he experiences the realities of life at an early age because of the fast pace of big city life. He is a product of his helicopter environment. Exposure to graffiti, shootings, gangs, peer pressure, poverty, negative influence, and all that is associated with living in the low-income housing projects. Being the only child had its challenges. Bullet holes are present on almost every street sign in the area. Helicopters fly around with its blinding spotlight, looking for gang members or fugitives that broke the law. Abandoned and deserted cars and trucks flood the poorly paved parking lot where residents lived. Oil stains are everywhere. Potholes so big that when you drive, you could easily break an axle if not careful. The strong smell of urine would cause you to go another direction. There is more trash piled up on the outside of the dumpsters than on the inside of the dumpster. Dirt trails leading from building to building is what people would constantly use, using the trails like ants in a colony traveling from place to place with its vast freeway system of life. Old sneakers would dangle from the utility lines that hung about twenty feet from the ground. The housing projects are run-down, and most of the buildings are neglected by the housing authority, neglected to the point where it seems as though they are inhumane. Seeing abandoned mattresses is not a perception; it is a telltale sign of reality. Graffiti painted as far as the eye could see was also a telltale sign of reality. The plumbing is shiesty, the electrical would work occasionally, and the sewage is not up to par. The children would run after the ice cream truck, once the old familiar sound that everyone knows is heard from a mile away.

Some residents make the most of the conditions by improvising what they have to support their families. You know times are hard when your neighbor would occasionally borrow sugar and eggs. Although the conditions were less than normal, when family would visit them, they would make living conditions comfortable by taking several layers of bed sheets and combining them to make a mattress, so that they would be comfortable. Relying on the government's assistance, they make the best to provide food to feed them. The appliances that are in the individual housing units do not perform as they should; for instance, the refrigerator would preserve the food for about one week as opposed to one month for those who could afford the latest and more sophisticated appliances.

Gangs use their influence to gain control of the people, both mentally and physically, to sustain their purpose to carry out whatever they want. Kidnapping, entitlement, influence, and control of what is rightfully theirs. Living in the projects has challenges all its own. Although Jasper was influenced by gangs, he never joined one. One of the problems is the lack of income that was scarce. His dad worked eight months in the year because of the line of work he is in: he works as a tradesman constructing small lease spaces which took about four to six months to build, and then he would move on to the next job which may be thirty to sixty miles from home. The car he has is a decent 1999 Buick Regal. It takes a lot of repairing, which is where most of the money is spent. The positive side to this is that his dad is a mechanic who saved the family some money. It is either spend the money for transportation, or have the state assist by being on welfare, which his dad and mom refuse to do.

Jasper's mom would take him down to the thrift store. The only privilege he has is to occasionally pick out some of his own clothing—if you want to call that privilege. This would happen when his clothes were too small, or in the fall season when it was time for school. There are no older siblings that he could depend on for hand-me-downs. He often begs his mom to get him a decent pair of name-brand sneakers. His hopes are slowly let down by a soft "no, we can't afford them" speech. He hoped that he would at least have a fair chance to avoid embarrassment if he had name-brand sneakers. Of course, this was wishful thinking on his part. Another thing that he dreaded was going to the laundromat with his mom. Carrying the heavy clothes from the car was one issue all itself. The other, on that note, far outweighed everything else: the fact that he was at the laundromat in the first place took the cake. Most everyone else had washers and dryers at the convenience of their homes.

This is the straw that breaks the camel's back. He is extremely embarrassed. While at school, Jasper tries to avoid any contact with his fellow classmates. He constantly looks around in all directions, making sure he is not seen.

Jasper is so determined not to be seen that it seems as though he is avoiding the plague. But despite all his efforts, he somehow runs into his classmates. A classmate named Dennis doesn't let him forget. This guy teases him every chance he gets, every time they cross paths. Dennis wants to accomplish two things: he wants to humiliate Jasper, and he wants to feed his ego at Jasper's expense. Jasper is a good kid, but he is not a pushover. He knows how to defend himself. He and Dennis would constantly have physical altercations. Jasper not only struggles with his embarrassment and hardship, but he also struggles with his grades, and something has to be done about it. Him and his parents continue to struggle. It has gotten to the point where money is so scarce that his parents had to decide to pay the light bill or put food on the table. This is something any parent would see as a nightmare. He would sometimes go to bed hungry because of the small portions of food he receives; this doesn't sit well with his parents. There is no doubt that a decision had to be made. Jasper would collect cans and turn them in for money, just enough for him to buy a couple of candy bars that he stashes in a cool place inside his closet. The candy bars would supplement his hunger cravings. His parents ponder for a few days, trying to find the best solution for him. So they decide to have him move with his aunt Dimple who is financially stable.

Chapter 2

Aunt Dimple

Jasper's aunt is in her mid-forties; she is not married and has no children. She has gone to church for most of her life. She sat in the pews at the back of the church. Over the years, she has decided to slowly move up one row at a time. It took her some time, but she finally made it to the front. She has struggles just like everyone else. Being in church for so many years and not having much to show lies heavy on her heart. Realizing that she is not bearing fruit is a concern. She decides to do something about it. Spending a lot of time on her knees talking to God changed her forever. She now has a new perspective of life, knowing how she has been blessed both physically and financially—the Lord has put it on her to help others like never before. She wants to make a difference, so she goes down to the county civil services adoption agency to get information about adopting two small children. The agency tells her that the children cannot be older than six years of age to be eligible for adoption. Because of the strict rules set forth by Los Angeles County, she is not eligible because of the hours she works. This discourages her, but the Lord tells her to be patient. One day she gets a phone call from Dottie, her sister. "Hey, sis, how things going?" Dottie asks.

"Blessed and doing well, you?" she responds.

"We're hanging in there barely, which is why I called you."

"What's going on?" Aunt Dimple asks.

"Well, you know I won't ask you for anything unless I absolutely have to. Jake and I have struggled to ask, but we want to know if you could take care of Jasper for us. We barely have enough to feed him. Both Jake and I have gotten to the point where we have had to literally give Jasper half the food from our plates, and it hasn't gotten any better," she explains.

"No worries, sis, I can do this for you—we can sit down and talk about this further in detail…that good for you?"

"Sure!" Dottie reacts as she sheds a tear. They all plan to meet at Aunt Dimple's house on the opposite side of the city the following week. The day has come: Dottie, Jake, and Jasper pull up in front of her home. The Buick coughs up a plume of smoke before Jake turns off the ignition. The houses close by have beautiful lawns that are mowed and sprinkler systems that are in full operation. People are walking their dogs, enjoying the warm sunshine. It appears that neighbors have no worries in the world. Jake looks around and makes a statement:

"I wouldn't mind having the problems they have at any given time on any given day." He gets out of the car and closes the door as he looks at his wife. Jake looks around and notices a brand-new Ford truck in the driveway of one of her neighbors.

"Man! That's nice—I'd love to have one of those." His wife looks back at him.

"I believe the Lord has a plan for us—this is only temporary, sweetheart." She, too, was brought up in the church but fell on hard times. Aunt Dimple prepares a meal for them. The menu consists of roasted chicken that she marinated overnight with fresh green beans and red potatoes, homemade mac and cheese, corn bread, and a tossed salad. Approximately thirty minutes pass by, and no one says a word except, "Would you please hand me that," the only words that are spoken at the time. After the meal they had Jasper go to another room to play video games or watch television while they talked. Jasper's mom and dad volunteer to help clean the kitchen.

Jasper's mom has something to say: "Sis, what I'm about to say comes from the heart. Jake and I have pondered on this for quite some time." She hesitates to speak.

"Go on, sis," Aunt Dimple expresses. A tear flows down her cheekbone. "We are short on money and having a difficult time taking care of Jasper."

She looks away in shame. "Let me step in, sweetheart," he says as he touches her on the shoulder gently. He continues, "What she's trying to say is that we sometimes go to bed with minimal food to eat. My company has restricted the hours that we work, and the odd jobs are not enough to support us all. So we want to ask if Jasper can stay with you until things turn around. It's hard to send our son to bed with his belly half full. When you look in his eyes, it's exceedingly difficult to tell him the truth of the matter. With that being said…will you be willing to help out?"

"Are you guys serious…help out! The time that people stop asking family for help is the time that everyone has become millionaires. Of course I'll help," Aunt Dimple replies.

Jasper's mom is beside herself. "God is always in control," she says.

She grabs her husband's hand and leads him outside to further express herself.

"Sis…give us a minute."

Once they get outside, she is the first to speak.

"Jasper living with his aunt couldn't have happened at a better time—God makes no mistakes. We must sit Jasper down and let him know about the decision we made and why."

Her husband responds, "I totally agree, sweetheart. Let's make sure that we explain it to him so that he won't rebel."

"That's a wonderful idea, sweetie, there is no better time to tell him than now."

"Again…I don't think we should sleep on this—I want sis to be involved in this conversation just in case she has something to add."

She tells him and he agrees. They walk back inside; they share the idea with her sister and ask her how she feels about her setting in on the conversation. Aunt Dimple agrees to sit in on the conversation.

All is well; Jasper gravitates to his aunt in no time. Once he settles in, he watches his aunt cook several food dishes in the kitchen, smelling the aroma day in and day out. He is curious to know how food is prepared and what is in food that makes it smell and taste so good. Every opportunity he got, he would make his way into the kitchen and watch his aunt go from the pantry to the cabinets to the refrigerator, gathering items that she deemed necessary to make such masterpieces.

ANTHONY S

Remember Jasper had very few cooked meals, so he not only appreciates them—he wants to learn how to prepare his own meals when that time arrives. She teaches him how to cook on the weekends when she has the time.

Like a roller coaster, this would continue for weeks or even months. When his parents would visit him, it was challenging for them. To see him brought them joy, but knowing that he could not come home with them was not a good thing emotionally. It is both a curse and a blessing all at the same time.

Jasper eventually sits by her bed and talks with her once he had built a certain trust and comfort. It has become a common thing for them both; it becomes a ritual. He does this until the age of fifteen; the ice is broken…

Chapter 3

Welcome

One day Jasper walks into his classroom and sees an unfamiliar face sitting at the back of the classroom. The guy that is sitting there appears to be lonely and intimidated by God knows what. Jasper has just walked in right before the tardy bell rings. His teacher asks everyone to sit in their assigned seats; once everyone is seated, she takes roll call. She calls everyone's name except the new guy.

"Is Roddie Wilson present?" she calls out.

He responds in a low voice, "Present, ma'am."

"Very well," she says.

Jasper sits in the third row from the front. He constantly looks over his shoulder to the back of the classroom, trying to figure out what Roddie is doing. Jasper notices that Roddie, who is fifteen, has something on his desk and is writing or drawing something. It's pretty obvious because his head lifts up every now and then. Jasper is curious and wants to know what Roddie is up to, so he deliberately gets out of his seat to sharpen his pencil. Jasper slowly walks past the new student to take a closer look. He gets close enough to see a drawing; it was impressive. Roddie looks up at him and makes a statement,

"I can teach you how to draw if you want me to," Jasper responds just in time before the teacher notices, and she calls them out.

"Would the two of you let the class know what the subject will be today?"

"No, ma'am," Jasper replies.

He looks at Roddie and makes a statement. "Meet you on the playground after school."

"Cool," Roddie says. The bells ring at 3:15 p.m. Both boys grabbed their backpacks and made their way to the playground. Roddie introduces himself in a formal fashion. Roddie tells him that he is a street artist that has recently moved there from Chicago.

"No worries, I'm Jasper from South Central, Los Angeles." They both laugh.

"Street artist, huh? You mean tagger or someone who paints graffiti," says Jasper.

"Yes…you must keep it a secret though," Roddie mentions. Roddie and Jasper agree to meet every day at the same place on the playground. It is getting too hot to draw outside for an extended period, so they eventually decide to meet at the public library. The library is four blocks away from the school. The library is quiet, and the boys would occasionally laugh aloud and are asked to leave by the librarian. The two of them are on a mission…they go from the playground to the library and eventually makes their way to Jasper's house.

"I'm sure my aunt wouldn't mind…she wants me to have someone that I can hang out with any way. I'll ask her if it's okay for us to draw in my room. I hope to have an answer for you tomorrow."

"You stay with your aunt?" Roddie asks.

"Yeah, it's a long story…I'll share it with you one day."

"Okay, cool, I'd like to hear it," he responds.

"Okay, Cool!" Jasper responds. They go on about their way. The following day they see each other in the classroom.

"Any word yet?" Roddie asks.

"Yes," Jasper responds. "She said it's okay, but she has to talk to your parents first."

Roddie gives Jasper his mom's cell phone number, so that his aunt can call to speak to Roddie's mom. Jasper continually asks his aunt if she called Roddie's parents. It seems to her like he would ask every hour on the hour. A couple of days have passed, and the boys see each other in the classroom as usual. "Anything?" Jasper asks.

"Yes, your aunt called my parents."

"Great!" Jasper says. It is finally settled; the necessary things have taken place for them to proceed. The two of them are on a mission…they go from the playground to the library, back and forth they go. The first time they met was over at Roddie's house. His room has posters of the latest action figures, some in 3D. He shows him all his previous drawings from when he lived in Chicago. Roddie's room was impressive…Jasper is overwhelmed at what he sees.

"I'm ready!" Roddie reaches under his mattress and takes out some construction paper and a board made of hardwood that his dad made for him. He also pulls out several #2 pencils and a pencil sharpener.

"Man, it doesn't get any better than this—I may as well spend the night!" Jasper yells. Roddie can't do anything but laugh. Roddie proceeds by showing him how to do simple outlines and shapes. Roddie will draw and then ask Jasper to draw exactly what he does. Jasper is a fast learner; Roddie goes from outlines to sketches. They continue to meet at Roddie's for a couple of weeks and then met over to Jasper's aunt's house for a couple of weeks. By the ninth week, Jasper has mastered most of the sketches that Roddie has previously drawn for him. Roddie would make things more challenging…he would occasionally put Jasper to the test. Roddie would randomly pick pictures for him to draw and give him a couple of days to finish drawing sketches of the pictures. Jasper never turned down any of his challenges; in fact, it had gotten to the point where he could draw a sketch of the same picture faster than Roddie could.

"Looks to me like you're ready to move on to color—are you ready?" Roddie asks him.

"Ready!" he responds. Roddie reaches inside his book bag and pulls out an assortment of colored pencils.

"Wow, you're full of surprises, buddy!" Jasper tells him. Roddie proceeds to hand him a few of the pencils. "I picked a picture, and we both must choose our own color to make it a masterpiece. Up for the challenge?" Roddie asks.

"Challenge is my middle name—let's do this!" Jasper responds with excitement.

"Okay, I have two of the same pictures. I'll take one and you take the other. We'll turn our backs to one another and start on our masterpieces. Ready?"

"You know, you keep asking me that—what gives you the idea that I'm not?" They both laugh. They begin to draw; Jasper finishes first.

"Man, you were fast—I thought I would win. I guess I was wrong." Roddie wants to teach him how to paint with aerosol cans. He makes plans for him and Jasper to meet at a secret location at a secluded place at the park. It can be a dangerous place because there are not a lot of people there—it's the perfect place for an opportunist. As a matter of fact, there are homeless people who occasionally sleep in this area; they always go together along with pocketknives…just in case. Off and on close to nine weeks, they cautiously head down to the park to paint masterpieces. Jasper is just as good with the aerosol cans as he is with colored pencils.

"Looks like you're ready to take it to the streets." Roddie assures him.

"Just so you know, I now have two skills—I am now a graffiti artist and cook," Jasper tells him.

"What do you mean?" he responds.

"Well, let's just say that I hang out in the kitchen with my aunt every now and then."

"You know how to cook? Man, that's cool." Roddie says.

"Just a little…I still have a long way to go, but I can hold my own," Jasper tells him. The teens select a time after school to go to the railyard and paint artwork, as they call it. They made sure that no one knew they were painting graffiti in public—this was their most sacred promise to one another; keeping it a secret. They both knew the consequences, they were very discreet as to who they disclosed their secret to. These teens drew almost every day, perfecting the art. Roddie educated Jasper about the dos and don'ts of painting in the railyard. He first tells him the dangers of painting on railcars.

"Don't ever walk in front of the engine where you can get trampled and run over. If it's attached to the railcars, it's a lot safer if you walk behind the last railcar. It's better to be dragged behind a car if you just happen to get your jacket or shirt caught on the railing of one of the cars. Trust me, you do not want either one, but one is a lot worse than the other. Painting can be a matter of life or death—it's the risk that we take…are you taking this all in, Jasper?"

"Yes! It sounds scary, but it seems worth the risk," Jasper responds.

"This is the life! Come on, follow me!" Roddie yells.

The young teens can appreciate yelling in the railyard because unlike school, they can yell and not get in trouble or be heard; the activity of the railyard during the day blocks out any potential noise; the trains make their own noise. They both grab their duffle bags with four to six aerosol cans of different colors and walk over to two new unmarked railcars that are sitting at the more secluded area of the railyard, minding their business.

"One more thing I must mention to you, make sure you don't paint on cars that are ready to mobilize," Roddie informs him.

"What do you mean mobilize?" he asks.

"It's a street word which means that a train is ready to move. Oh, you'll know! When the railcars are attached to one another, and you hear a loud noise that makes you grab your ears and scares the hell out of you, then that's when you'll know." Roddie assures him.

"Man, I don't know about this—are you sure?" Jasper asks.

"Yes, I'm sure if you remember all the things I've told you, you should be fine—as I said before, the thrill is greater than the risk."

"Okay, let's do this!" For almost two hours each day after school, they would take their aerosol cans and paint the most beautiful artwork that a teen had to offer. Sometimes they would get carried away and stay until it was almost dark. There were several occasions when they would have to explain themselves for coming home late.

Chapter 4

CONVICTION OF THE HEART

Jasper and his aunt Dimple attend church quite often. This day as they head home from church, he strikes up a conversation with her. He tells her that he likes to paint with colored pencils, paint brushes, and aerosol cans.

She responds, "That's a great hobby for a young man to have."

Jasper says, "Well, Aunt Dimple, I trust that I can talk to you about anything…correct?"

She answers, "Correct—what's on your mind, dear?"

"Well, it's not quite the art that you expect. It's not like drawing on a piece of paper. It's more like drawing on different objects with an aerosol can." He continues to explain what it is that he likes to do in detail.

"I have mixed emotions. Going to church with you and painting on objects—it just seems like the two just don't go together," he further explains.

She says to him, "What you feel is conviction of the heart about what is right and what is wrong—that's not a bad thing. You have been with me for eight months and you're already maturing in the Lord. This is a prime example of the more you're engaged in something, the more you understand and master it."

"You mean like painting?" he asks.

"Yes…sort of—that's not the point I was trying to make, but sort of…you are really beginning to understand things and see things more clearly, young man. I think it's time to call your parents—it's been a while since you had spoken to them." She didn't expect Jasper would tell her what he just did; she was shocked. She responds with a gesture as she slowly veers into another lane.

"I have one more thing to tell you, auntie," he says.

She responds, "What more could there be? I thought I heard it all."

"Now that you know of my friend Roddie, I want you to know that we paint street art together," he explains.

"Oh, Lord, not one but two—have mercy on them, Lord!" They both laugh. "Sure, I would like to meet the young man. Can you find out if he's available to come over this weekend?" She asks.

"Yes, I can call him to see." He calls Roddie as soon as they make it home from church.

"Hey, dude, whatcha up to?" Jasper asks.

"I just got home from church."

"Church…what's that?" Roddie asks.

"It's a cool place to go to get to know Jesus."

"Who is Jesus?" Jasper continues to explain who Jesus is. "Wow! He seems to be a pretty cool dude."

"He's not a dude—he's a spirit. I'll tell you more later. Well, I was just talking to my aunt about you, and she wants to meet you."

"Sure! Wait…she's nothing like my dad, is she?"

"No…in fact, she's just the opposite!" Jasper assures him.

Aunt Dimple finally meets his friend Roddie and takes a liking to him. They show her some of their drawings, and she is impressed with their work. Even though Jasper goes to church, he still struggles with a few things, like we all do. One day while Jasper is in his room preparing for school, he decides to throw a couple of paint cans inside his book bag. He grabs his lunch off the counter, his door key and sets the alarm. He then heads for the back door. He normally met Roddie at school, but he decides to take a detour. A new office building is under construction and is nearly finished. Jasper has previously noticed the building while it was under construction for a couple of months now.

He could not avoid the temptation of stopping by and taking a closer look at the progress that's been constructed thus far. He finds a good spot on the side of the building.

He looks around to make sure the coast is clear. He retrieves the paint cans from his book bag and paints a beautiful picture of Jesus—he's in a zone for sure. Jasper has been painting on the building now for about thirty minutes. He is interrupted by a tap on the horn of a vehicle. He turns around and notices a policeman sitting in his patrol car. The police officer sits there for a minute before he gets out. By this time Jasper's heart is beating rapidly as the officer approaches him. The officer yells out "Put the paint cans down, young man!"

Jasper is beside himself, so instead of putting the paint cans down, he just drops them on the ground where he stood. "You better not run! Or I'll pull out my taser."

Jasper responds, "Yes, officer," as he throws his hands in the air. By the way, the officer is atheist and hard-core.

"Who is that?" the officer yells.

"It's a picture of Jesus, sir."

"Jesus! Who the hell is Jesus?" Before Jasper could answer, the officer takes his handcuffs and quickly places them on Jasper's wrists. "Let's go! These handcuffs will take the place of Jesus for now. Let's see if this Jesus can get you out of these cuffs!" Although Jasper wants to tell the officer that Jesus can do anything he wants, including taking off the cuffs, he just simply realizes that he's not in the position to do so. So he is reserved and stays quiet. He realizes that the officer doesn't know or like Jesus. Jasper is taken down to the police precinct.

Meanwhile, Roddie is trying to call him because he is thirty minutes late for school. Jasper is not answering his phone because the officer has taken it from him. Jasper is being booked at the station. He is put in an individual jail cell temporarily because he is a minor. They ask him where his parents are. He tells them that he lives with his guardian aunt. They in turn ask him for a contact number. Once they get the cell number, they don't hesitate to call her. Aunt Dimple is at work at the time she receives the call. She answers the call. "Hello, this is Dimple. How may I help you?"

The officer responds, "This is the Los Angeles police department—is this Mrs. Montgomery?"

She responds, "Yes, it is, may I help you?" The officer tells her why he is calling, and she is in a daze for about ten seconds. She takes her cell and walks outside. "Ma'am, are you there?"

"Yes, may I speak to him?" She gives Jasper an earful and asks him what he was thinking. Jasper is at a loss of words. She asks to speak back to the officer. Jasper slowly hands the phone back to the officer. The officer tells her that she has to pick him up from the station and that he has to face the judge on a later date. She goes to her desk and finishes what she is doing. She then goes to her supervisor to tell him that she has to leave for the day. This situation with Jasper has thrown her way off balance; it constantly stays on her mind. She rarely misses work and never leaves early.

Grabbing her belongings, she heads straight to her car. The entire time that she is driving, she anticipates exactly what she is going to say to him. She is also thinking about how her sister and brother-in-law will react once they hear about this. As she is driving, she gradually calms down to a reasonable level. Continuing to drive to the police station, the Lord speaks to her. He reminds her that we all fall short of his glory and that we were born in sin. He also gives her peace of mind as he reminds her to forgive.

She is calm when she arrives at the police station. It takes her twenty-five minutes to get there. As she walks to the entrance of the station, she is thinking, *Forgiveness, forgiveness, forgiveness.* She walks inside and heads to the receptionist and asks for Jasper and tells the receptionist who she is. The receptionist asks her for her ID and proof of guardianship. Aunt Dimple reaches in her purse and gives the receptionist all that she needs. "Give me a moment—please take a seat," the receptionist says.

"Sure, thank you," Aunt Dimple responds as she looks around for a place to sit. It doesn't take long for the receptionist to return to the front counter. She tells Aunt Dimple to sign a few papers and tells her that Jasper will receive a court date in the mail. In return, the receptionist hands her a few papers that have instructions on them. The receptionist then instructs her to go down the hallway to a section where minors are in holding cells. When she gets there, she talks to an officer who is standing at the entrance. The officer goes through another door to get Jasper and bring him to the front. Aunt Dimple waits there patiently as she stares at the television. Jasper and the officer approach her. "Thanks, officer," she says. She turns and looks at Jasper. "Young man, I want you to tell me exactly what you were thinking," she says as they begin walking down the hallway and back to the car.

Jasper has his head down, looking at the shiny ceramic tiles, counting them as he walks. He gets to the fourth one before he begins to speak. "Sorry, Auntie, don't know exactly what I was thinking! I saw an opportunity, and temptation overtook me! I sincerely apologize. I feel bad that you had to come from work to pick me up!"

"Well, don't beat yourself up too bad. I forgive you—that's what we're supposed to do anyway." You would have thought it was the last day of school the way he lit up; this is not what he expected. He looks at her in amazement and sheds a tear. Before they reach the car, he hugs her… in return she hugs him.

"Don't forget this is not over—you still must go to court and face the judge. I pray that the judge has sympathy. I will be there with you, and so will the Lord." She assures him.

When they get inside the car and continue to drive, she makes a statement: "I won't tell your mom or dad about this—I don't want them to get riled up. They have enough to worry about. Since I am your guardian, I will take matters into my own hands."

Jasper responds, "Thanks, Auntie, what a relief!" Jasper is anxious so he calls Roddie. He tells Roddie that he will tell him everything when they get to school tomorrow. Jasper wants to eat, take a shower, and relax for the rest of the day. He has a lot on his mind. The next morning when he wakes up, the thought is still with him. He goes through the same routine: grabbing his lunch, book bag, and keys, he heads for the back door to go to school. Jasper decides to go back to the crime scene to reflect on his drawing, but it is no longer there. He stands there for a few minutes, then walks a few blocks over to his bus stop, thinking the entire time.

Chapter 5

MERCY

When Jasper gets to school, he goes to his normal hangout. Roddie is there waiting on him. "Man, what happened!" Roddie asks.

"You won't believe what I've been through!" Jasper breaks down every moment, detail by detail. Once it's all said and done, Roddie stands there with his mouth wide open… giving a potential fly the perfect opportunity. Jasper and

Roddie continue their routine, anticipating the arrival of his court date. It doesn't take but a few days for his court appointment to arrive in the mail. Aunt Dimple retrieved it from the mail, reads it, and puts it on Jasper's bed. That afternoon when Jasper got home, he goes straight to the fridge to grab a cold drink and heads to his room. He immediately notices a white envelope sitting on his pillow. He has an idea where the letter came from and what it was about. He slowly picks it up and notices that the letter has been opened by someone. The letter is brief and to the point; he reads it.

It read: Jasper Smith is in violation of penal code #334, vandalism of public property, and is summoned to appear in juvenile court before honorable Judge Rose Simpson. The date is set for March thirteenth at 10:30 a.m. Your guardian Mrs. Montgomery must be present as well. Respectfully, the Los Angeles County Juvenile Court Division.

Reality has just kicked down his door. Aunt Dimple calls him on his cell phone not long after. She figures that he would be home by this time. He answers his cell phone. "Hello, Aunt Dimple."

She responds, "Hey, you, did you get the letter that I put on your bed?"

"Yes, I did," he says. Anxiety has taken affect; it was inevitable that he must face the judge, but reality has just become real to him. He's a little shaken up at this point. Aunt Dimple can hear it in his voice.

"I suggest you go to a quiet room, get down on your knees, and pray to our Heavenly Father. It may not turn out as bad as you think. You must have faith in Him for the outcome to be favorable." Now that Jasper has a confirmed court date, Aunt Dimple decides to take off work and take Jasper out of school so that he doesn't miss seeing the judge.

The day of court, Jasper and Aunt Dimple arrive at the courthouse downtown. The parking lot is expensive and congested. The elevator takes them to the fourth floor; this is where they walk through metal detectors. Jasper's heart is pounding more than usual. One of the Bailiffs briefly looks through Aunt Dimple's purse while the other Bailiff directs Jasper to stand nearby. Once they go through the detectors, the Bailiff looks at the summons that Aunt Dimple is holding in her hand. The Bailiff directs them to the correct courtroom. They go inside two huge wooden doors. The Bailiff tells them to take a seat and that the judge will call them.

As they enter quietly, there is another case that the judge is overseeing. By this time, Jasper is so afraid that it seems as though his heart stopped beating. One would think that he would snatch the nearby defibrillator off the wall and make use of it. "Aunt Dimple, is it hot in here, or is it just me?" he asks.

"No, sweetheart, it's just you. I can only imagine how you may feel. Go grab a sip of water and relax," she replies. Jasper gets up and struggles to make it out to the hallway where the water fountains are located. He then heads to the bathroom. He walks over to the sink, splashes water on his face, and grabs a paper towel. He walks toward the bathroom door, grabs the door handle, and takes a deep breath before opening it. Jasper goes back into the courtroom, and not long after, the judge calls his name.

"Jasper Smith, would you approach the bench!" He looks around the courtroom as though there is maybe another Jasper Smith. The judge notices what he does and gestures him to come forward. Others watch as he slowly walks down the aisle. He finally reaches the bench; he just stands there with his hands to his sides with a plain look on his face. The judge reads his violation aloud. The judge asks to see the evidence in question. The lead Bailiff instructs another Bailiff to retrieve the photos from a keep safe place in the back. For the first time, the judge sees the photos. Judge Simpson is blown away when she sees what he drew a picture of. She takes the pictures and sits them down. She steps down from the bench and walks over to Jasper.

"I want to see you in my chambers, young man."

Jasper is beside himself. "Ma'am, can my aunt come with me?"

"Sure, she can come along." The judge responds. The judge walks toward her chambers and instructs one bailiff to escort Jasper and his aunt to her chambers as well. She further instructs the bailiff to stay outside the door as she talks to Jasper. Once inside, Judge Simpson explains why she wants them in her chambers. She is impressed with his drawings.

"You are such a great artist! This is extremely rare for a person your age to draw a picture of our Lord and Savior."

"My aunt Dimple told me about Him!"

"Don't get me wrong—I have to uphold the law, but what you have painted is nothing short of amazing."

"I know that painting on the walls is illegal, but this is all I know," Jasper expresses.

"Well, I'm blown away! So let me tell you what I plan to do. I will not let you do jail time. What I will do is…have you pay a fine for vandalism, and you will also serve in the community after school or on the weekends—your choice. I'm telling you this, so that you know what to expect once we get back into the courtroom. I must disclose this same information in front of the court. I believe in you. Don't get caught because I have to give you a more severe punishment the next time around, even if I don't want to."

She looked at Aunt Dimple and smiles. She looks at Jasper and winks her eye. "God is merciful!" says Aunt Dimple.

"Yes, he is," Judge Simpson responds. Jasper has tears in his eyes. The judge wishes him well and instructs them to go back into the courtroom. As long as Jasper finishes community service and pays all the fines, then he would clear his name and began to build the trust of his aunt again.

"Auntie, I would like to reach out to others somehow—I want them to know about Jesus also."

"Do you have any idea how you would like to make this possible?" she asks.

"Well, I'm not really sure," he says. "Why don't you use the gift that God has anointed you with?" she asked him.

"What gift, Auntie?"

"You mean you really have to ask? I don't approve of you painting graffiti, but…"

He quickly interrupts her. "We don't paint graffiti, Auntie—we call it street art."

"Well, whatever," she responds with a playful gesture. She continues, "Seriously, I think you should somehow use the gift that you were given in a positive way—not exactly sure how, but I think you'll figure something out."

He shouts with excitement, "I have an idea—why don't I paint images of Jesus all over the city! Auntie what do you think?"

"Well, I have mixed feelings about you painting on objects around the city, and this would be considered vandalism to most people, but God said to go into the world and spread the Gospel of Christ, but he never said how to go about it. That might not be such a bad idea after all. Considering how corrupt the world is nowadays, I'd say go for it—the lesser of the two evils…I can't believe I am condoning this… God help us. Like Judge Simpson said, don't get caught."

After Jasper and Aunt Dimple arrived home, he immediately picks up his cell phone and calls Roddie; Roddie answers, "Man! I thought they had given you twenty years!"

"Not quite! I have a question for you," Jasper says.

"Shoot!"

"What's the scariest movie you've ever seen?"

"Man! There's a few…let's see, how 'bout the movie *Quarantine*? I didn't sleep for a week…why do you ask?"

"Well, watching that movie was equal to how I felt in the courtroom," Jasper explains.

"Wow, what did the judge say?"

"Let's just say I don't have to do jail time."

"Man, you got off easy. I'm sure it wasn't your charm," Roddie tells him.

"No, the judge liked the painting of Jesus that I painted," Jasper explains.

"Wow!"

Jasper continues to fill Roddie in on the details.

Chapter 6

BREAKING THE ICE

At the ages of fifteen and sixteen, they both mastered the art of graffiti, aka street art, as they call it. One day as Aunt Dimple is heading to work, she notices the painting of a dove on the side of a building located at the park. Although she isn't sure, she assumes it was Jasper's painting. She continues to drive to work when an idea pops inside her head: "I wonder if Jasper would like to paint pictures on canvas backboards, display them, and sell them to the public. We can even sell some of his paintings at the church. I will pay for the things he needs to get him started. This will enable him properly to manage his money. Teach him to be responsible and prioritize what is important and what is not important when it comes to spending money. This will help him in the future. What a wonderful idea—I will run this by Jasper and speak to the pastor about my idea as well."

Jasper and Roddie buy things in bulk when they get their paychecks. Things such as: paint cans, rags, paint thinner, colored pencils, pencil sharpeners, backpacks, gloves, paint brushes, etc. Roddie needed to suppress the abuse he received from his father. His father would frequently tell him to paint the house if he really wanted to paint. He hung out with Jasper 95 percent of the time. It is apparent to Aunt Dimple and Jasper that Roddie deliberately stays a while longer on most days. It has gotten to the point where Aunt Dimple insists that he go home to avoid trouble from his dad. Jasper is always reluctant to go see Roddie because his dad is stern and intimidating. Sometimes when Jasper goes over to Roddie's, he would either call or go to the back door to avoid his dad.

"Now that you met my aunt, you can hang out over here more often to keep your mind off of your dad."

"That's a temp fix, bro…I was hoping I could move in!" They both laugh. "On the serious note my dad is under pressure since my step-mom moved away and his job demands more from him. I want to make him proud of me somehow by helping more on the bills. I can't make it on $8 an hour part-time. I need a way to make some quick cash!"

"I want to do the same. My aunt has the means, but I don't want to always burden her—besides, I want to get the latest sports jacket and shoes to match! Ya dig?"

"Dude, I hear you loud and clear!" The following day they both meet up at their usual hangout at school. They always have two bags with them most of the time. One of the bags is for school and the other bag carries all the things needed to paint street art just in case. If they spot a clean surface and it is in unchartered territory and the opportunity presents itself, then they make the best of it.

Principal Davenport notices the boys and walks over to them. "Morning, gentlemen, why is it that you have two backpacks each?"

Roddie answers before Jasper could open his mouth. "Principal Davenport, we have these bags with us because we have a hobby that we do—after school, of course."

"Well, I must check the bags for security reasons."

They give him all the bags and he searches for any weapons or items that are not fit for school. "I don't see any weapons, or things of concern, but these paint cans are an entirely different story. If I don't see any paintings here on campus, then we're good to go. Meanwhile, I need you gentlemen to keep the bag with the paint cans in your lockers and the ones with the books on your shoulders. Thanks, gentlemen."

Jasper responds, "Will do, sir!" Principal Davenport sees students smoking and heads their way.

"I noticed that you always paint the picture of Jesus, or some sort of dove or cross or something of that nature—why is that?" Roddie asks.

"As long as I'm alive, I will always honor our Lord and Savior. It's my way of showing the world who he is: the hope of mankind. Jesus protects us, provides for us, encourages us, loves us. My Aunt Dimple has instilled in me that we are to be disciples of Jesus and spread the Gospel."

"What does that mean?" Roddie asks.

Jasper continues, "That means that we are all supposed to witness and tell others how Jesus died for our sins.

He comforts others, giving them hope to change sinful ways—it's called repenting. I spread the word with my drawings, others have other ways…this is the one I chose."

"Man, that's deep!" Roddie responds. "Man, I don't know what I'd do if it weren't for you and Aunt Dimple. Speaking of family my dad called me in his room last night. He told me that he was addicted to pain meds from an injury he experienced years ago. He explained why he acts the way he does. He told me that he must tell me in case something were to happen to him. Dude! He finally opened up to me."

Jasper responds, "That's awesome, dude! Maybe he is feeling the conviction of the Holy Spirit and not even know it…it's called intervention. I would love to go see him and pray with him. Can you tell him that I would like to pray for him?"

"Man, my dad has confided in me, and I don't want that to change—he might not be cool with that. Let's just let dead dogs lie for a while," Roddie says.

"I'm cool with that, but you still haven't had the opportunity to ask him—that's not fair to him. The Bible says we are to leave no man behind. Think about it…that's the reason I paint pictures of inspiration to reach out to those who don't know Jesus. When they see the paintings, hopefully, they will seek him, find out who he is, and go from there. All I'm doing is fulfilling the very thing that I do in my paintings," Jasper expresses.

"Dude, you get it! So right, bro…I'll ask him—besides, you are my best friend, and he should understand that the intention behind praying for him is nothing short of compassion."

"Exactly!" Jasper expresses. "I truly believe we should do this sooner than later," Jasper continues.

"I'm on it—I'll talk to him as soon as I get home today."

"Great, keep me posted," Jasper tells Roddie. As soon as Roddie got home, he talked to his dad. Surprisingly, Roddie's dad was not upset when he heard that Jasper wants to pray for him. In fact, he had nothing to lose. When the time came to pray for his father, both Roddie and Jasper were there.

"It's been a while, son. Jasper, Roddie can't seem to stay away from you. I can't say that's a bad thing. I have noticed a change in him. He seems to be coming around. You are a positive influence in my son's life, and I just want him to be able to survive in this crazy, selfish, and uncertain world that we live in."

"Yes, sir, me and Roddie are the best of friends, and I don't mind praying for you, sir. Shall we?" Jasper expresses.

He asks Roddie to hold his hand and his father's hand. Jasper asks everyone to close their eyes and bow their heads. Jasper says a very sincere prayer and makes sure that every word that comes from his mouth is clear and concise. The prayer is long and precise. Roddie and Jasper leave the house not long after. His dad feels the Holy Spirit to the point where he finds his Bible stored away somewhere in the house and sits it on his nightstand beside his bed. He makes it a priority to read it from time to time.

"Say, bro, let's go check out that new ice cream spot down the street—you down?" Jasper asks Roddie.

"You ain't said nothin' but a word—let's go!" Roddie and Jasper walk down the street. They pass by the storefront window of an appliance store. The store has a bunch of televisions for sale that are on display. Several of the televisions are turned on to the local news channels.

"Dude, look!" Roddie gets Jasper's attention as he points to one of the televisions. The news channel shows one of the paintings that Jasper painted. They walk inside the store to listen to what the news anchor has to say.

The news anchor covers the story: "*I am standing here in front of one of many paintings from around the city. This particular one is a painting of the Messiah that someone apparently has painted. Officials are wondering if the paintings have a direct impact of the reduction of crime in the city. Whoever this anonymous person is may have a motive behind the paintings. This raises many questions. The purpose of the drawings—can this be a message that we all must take heed to? Could this continue to impact our community? One must wonder. This is Merian Jenkins reporting…Channel 13 News.*"

Chapter 7

LIFELINES

Roddie and Jasper are in their last year of school. They plan to meet at the usual location. It's 4:00 p.m. and there are students everywhere. The school bell rang fifteen minutes ago. It's late spring, but today there is an overcast of clouds.

"Hey, man, this is our last year in school—let's make the best of it! There is only one negative thing. I try to please that man in any way possible, and he doesn't appreciate anything I do," Roddie expresses.

"You don't mean your father, do you?"

"Yes," Roddie answers.

"Man, I thought y'all were cool!" Jasper expresses. Roddie continues to tell him how he felt about his dad. "I remember you saying that you were willing to help by getting a job to show that you are responsible and wanted to help pay bills. Did I miss something?" Jasper asks.

"Dude! I don't know what his problem is…I give up!"

"Can I speak freely bro?" Jasper asks.

"What's up, bro?" he responds.

Jasper tells Roddie about his own life's experiences. "I have been through it all, bro. Since my parents sent me to stay with Aunt Dimple, I became a different person. At first, I despised my parents for doing it, but later realized that they wanted the best for me. With that being said, maybe your dad may not know how to love. Give him a chance and see what happens next before you throw in the towel. Turn the other cheek, as our Heavenly Father said we should do…I have!"

Roddie responds, "Man! That's deep! I'm willing to try once more!" Jasper continues to explain the importance of forgiving your fellow man to Roddie. Roddie receives this advice with gratitude.

"Say, bro, let's enjoy our last year of school doing something different…I have something that I want to share with you. I really need you to come to the railyard this coming Sunday…you down?" Roddie asks Jasper.

"Would love to!" Jasper says with excitement.

"Cool, and thanks for the advice, bro." Roddie tells Jasper. Roddie ponders on every word that Jasper spoke. Both Jasper and Roddie go on with life as usual until Sunday arrives.

It's Sunday, and they plan to meet at the railyard at 1:00 p.m. The railyard is full of railcars and diesel engines. The railyard is not completely quiet; however, there are a few squeaks and squills from the very few railcars that employees are moving to various tracks. The rail workers prepare the railyard for the next shift of workers that would start work at 7:00 a.m. that Monday morning. "Here we are, buddy!" Roddie tells Jasper.

"What are you up to?" Jasper asks.

"Let's take our street art to the next level. I want to show you something that I came up with." He grabs his backpack and pulls out a can of paint. "I want to introduce you to the new concept of lifelines."

"That sounds serious…what are lifelines?"

"Let's just say that lifelines are something that I thought of, and I want both of us to experience together. Yes, it's serious and dangerous!" Roddie explains the concept to Jasper: he tells Jasper that they would both take a can of paint and spray railcars as they are moving. The idea is to paint lines on the railcars which are like the ones on the monitors in the emergency rooms of hospitals.

"Let me caution you. Before we start, we must make it a law to take off anything that may get caught on any part of the train such as our jackets, jewelry, backpacks, etc. Are you down? If so, follow me."

"If you're crazy enough to do it, then I'm crazy enough to join you," Jasper says.

Roddie tells Jasper, "It will definitely be a rush of adrenaline—follow me!" Roddie takes the lead and picks out a railcar that is heading in their direction.

"I'll go first," says Roddie. "We must paint the slower trains and gradually make our way up to the faster trains." He grabs a can of blue spray paint from his backpack and drops his backpack on the ground. He approaches the slow-moving train and begins to spray in an up-and-down motion with quick reflexes. As the train moves forward, they can see the blue lines clearly.

"Not bad for the first time," says Jasper.

"Totally agree, bro, you're up!"

Jasper takes a paint can from his backpack. He then takes off his watch and puts it in the backpack and sits it on the ground. He and Roddie both look for another slow-moving train. "There's one, bro!" Jasper yells. Roddie grabs both backpacks and follows Jasper as he runs after the railcar. Jasper reached the railcar and begins to paint on it. He does the same thing that Roddie had done previously. Once he finishes, he looks at the passing railcar until it moves around the curved tracks. He watches until he can't see the railcar anymore.

"Dude! That was awesome! I can get the hang of this!" Jasper says.

"Yeah, me and you both!" They stay for a couple of hours before heading home. The following day, they met at the usual hangout after school. "Man! Yesterday was off the chain."

"Yes, it was—let's not tell anyone about our new adventure. As a matter of fact…let's make this a ritual and do this every Saturday instead of Sunday. This is the very thing I need to keep my dad off my mind…you down?" Roddie asks.

"Speaking of Sunday, Aunt Dimple would like for you to go to church with us and invite you over for dinner afterward. If possible, she wants to know by Friday, so that she can go to the grocery store and pick up a few items for Sunday's dinner," Jasper tells him. "I told her that you were continuing to make things right with your dad and how difficult he has been. I normally wouldn't get her involved, but I thought it was necessary. Hope you understand, bro."

"Dude, I'm not mad at cha—it's not like you have ulterior motives. You're only looking out for my well-being—that's what friends do. As a matter of fact…thanks, bro!"

"Welcome, bro!" They bump elbows and give one another a quick hug.

"Okay, back to the church thing. I have never been to church—how do I act? What do I wear?" Roddie expresses.

"Do you have any slacks or dress shoes?" Jasper asks.

Roddie responds, "Nah, all I have is jeans, T-shirts, and tennis shoes. My jeans have holes that I cut in them."

"Well, let me ease your mind. Jesus wants all people to come as they are. There is no certain dress code. He is interested in our salvation, not our appearance."

"What's salvation?" Roddie asks.

Jasper explains, "Salvation is when our physical body dies our souls/spirit must go somewhere—either hell or heaven. It's strictly our choice. Our Heavenly Father gives us that choice free willingly. Believe me you don't want to go to hell…it's eternal damnation with no relief."

"Man, that sounds cruel—actually, that's pretty darn scary. How do you avoid eternal damnation?"

"There is only one way," Jasper says.

"Man, you have my undivided attention!"

Jasper continues, "Our Heavenly Father wants us to acknowledge in our hearts and minds and fully accept the fact that his son Jesus has died for the sins of mankind."

"Is that all? Man, sign me up!" Roddie expresses.

"The sad thing is that a lot of people have not or will not accept this," Jasper says.

"What! Why not?" Roddie asks.

"Not sure, bro, maybe pride—most people feel as though they don't need anyone to help them with anything including salvation…I guess. With no hesitation, I have accepted Jesus as my Lord and Savior. Will you?"

"Well, yeah!" Roddie yells. "Can you help me do this?"

"Sure, thing buddy."

"This might sound a little weird—let's go to a quiet place."

They find a quiet place on school ground. "I'm going to place my hand on your shoulder—repeat after me." He says a few words, and Roddie repeats them.

"Dude, I felt some type of relief as I repeated every word you said…it was a great feeling!" Roddie expresses.

"It was the Holy Spirit…you're good ta go!"

Roddie's eyes begin to water. "Man, I felt at peace for a moment—it took my mind off of things. I can't thank you enough, bro! Make sure you tell Aunt Dimple that I will be there Sunday morning, ready for church!"

"Will do!" Jasper tells him.

"Cool! I will see you Sunday, bro, call me and let me know what time I should be at your place so I can be prepared," Roddie expresses.

"Will do." They both go their separate ways. Later that evening, Jasper talks to Aunt Dimple.

"I am fond of that young man. I don't like the fact that he has issues with his father the way that he has. I want to pray with him on Sunday. I'm looking forward."

"I think that's an awesome idea, Aunt Dimple. I'm sure he'll like that, as a matter of fact I need to call him. What time should Roddie be here Sunday?"

Aunt Dimple responds, "Yes, that's important—ask him to be here by 9:00 a.m."

"Okay, Aunt Dimple, will do." Jasper goes to his room and calls Roddie.

"Sup, bro! Aunt Dimple asked you to be here Sunday by 9:00 a.m."

"Cool, I don't know why I'm so excited."

"Bro, as I told you…it's the Holy Spirit that you're experiencing."

"Man, I like the Holy Spirit! He gives me peace!"

"Well yeah, that is exactly what he does! You are right on time! Seems to me that you're going to be okay! I'll see you Sunday."

The phone call ends, and Roddie stands there for a moment and takes it all in. He can't believe that despite how his dad treats him, there are still people who care about him. Jasper is also excited about Roddie coming to church with them. Jasper talks to Aunt Dimple a while longer. He decided to go to his room and pick out some nice attire for the coming Sunday.

Roddie calls Jasper back immediately; he wants to share a thought that is on his mind. Roddie says to Jasper, "Seems wrong to paint on objects in the public."

Jasper tells him, "I felt the same way. I put things into perspective though. I feel like the world should know Jesus. I want to fulfil his purpose. It's not like we're painting gang signs." Roddie totally agrees.

Jasper tells Aunt Dimple, "I believe Roddie is coming along. He now knows who Jesus is, and now he will experience His manifestation. His dad doesn't have a negative influence on him anymore."

Chapter 8

GLOW

It's six o'clock on Sunday morning. Roddie's cell phone vibrates on the nearby table. His alarm wakes him. He hits the snooze button two times before he gets out of bed; he's excited. He turns on the iron and waits a few minutes while the iron gets to its desired temperature. He takes his pre-ironed clothes and hit them again, making sure there are no visible wrinkles present. He grabs a clean pair of socks and underwear and walks down the hallway to the bathroom. He notices that his dad is still sleeping. He realizes this because his dad's bedroom door is closed. By law, if his door is closed, that clearly means that he is tired and doesn't want to be bothered. He works the third shift usually from 10 p.m. to 7 a.m. If Roddie takes a bat and hits the wall with it, his dad wouldn't budge. Roddie gets dressed, walks into the kitchen, gets two sausage biscuits, and puts them in the microwave for a couple of minutes. He walks to the fridge and pours himself a tall glass of orange juice. He takes a jar of grape jelly and sits it on the kitchen table. He plays it safe by grabbing a couple of paper towels and tucks them inside the neck of his shirt, making sure that no jelly accidently falls on his neatly ironed shirt.

The night before, he made sure that the buses ran early. This would allow him to factor in his travel time. He has never caught the bus that early in the morning on Sunday. When Roddie finishes his breakfast, he takes a pen and notepad and writes his dad a note and slides it under his dad's bedroom door. There is one privilege that his dad will grant him: freedom to come and go as he pleases if Roddie takes care of things around the house first. Roddie quietly takes his cell phone, keys, and wallet and puts them in his pockets. He makes sure that he has his pre-paid bus pass. He checks to make sure all the doors are locked before he exits the house.

It's close to 7:20 a.m. It takes him ten minutes to walk to the nearest bus stop. When he gets to the bus stop, he calls Jasper on his cell phone. "Sup, bro! Are you ready?" Roddie asks with excitement.

"Yes, I'm just about finished getting dressed. Dude, you are hype!"

"Well, I have every reason to be. Once you told me about Jesus, I was sold the very first time!"

"Awesome!" Jasper expresses.

Roddie notices that the bus is headed his way. "All right, bro, see you in a bit. The bus is coming."

"Cool, looking forward," Jasper tells him. He takes a seat at the very back of the bus. He passes an older lady as he walks by.

"Young man, you look nice and fresh," the lady says.

"Yes, ma'am, I'm going to church for the first time."

"That's not a bad thing at all—I'm a believer in Christ as well. Let's continue to pray for one another and make sure we reach out to others. I wish you well, young man. God bless."

"Thanks for the encouraging words, ma'am…God bless." Roddie takes his seat and reflects on Jasper and what he said about spreading the word. *Wow*, he thinks to himself: *Jasper is spreading the word by painting pictures of Jesus all over the city. That's amazing how things are lining up—it's starting to make sense to me.* Roddie sits on the bus for a few minutes, pondering. He arrives at the intersection of Blake and Addison. He reaches up to pull the rip cord, so that the bus driver knows where his next stop would be.

After the bus stops, he gets off and walks to Jasper's house. He walks up the sidewalk and rings the doorbell. Jasper answers the door.

"Sup, dude," Roddie says.

"Let's do something a little different this time. Let's just say good morning, bro…how does that sound?" Jasper asks him.

"I can handle that," Roddie responds. They walk inside the house. Aunt Dimple sees Roddie as he walks through the door.

"Morning, young man. I'm so glad that you made it and it's great to see you."

"Morning, Aunt Dimple, it's great to be here. I am eager to go to church with you and Jasper. I consider you all family."

"Well, that's exactly what you are," Aunt Dimple responds.

"You hungry?"

"No, ma'am—I already had breakfast, but I could go for another glass of orange juice. I had one glass this morning."

"Coming right up." She walks into the kitchen as Roddie and Jasper talk.

"Bro, you clean up pretty nice." Jasper tells him.

"So do you, bro—we look like we both make twenty dollars an hour." They both laugh and fist bump. Aunt Dimple returns with the orange juice and hands the glass to Roddie.

TAGGER

"Thanks, Aunt Dimple." Roddie says.

"Welcome, dear…Jasper, breakfast is ready. Roddie, you can join us in the kitchen if you'd like. We have forty minutes to eat before we leave for church. The plan is to get there early so that we can get a good parking spot—it's always crowded on Sundays. Let's say grace."

Aunt Dimple blesses the food and has small talk as they enjoy each other's company. After breakfast, Aunt Dimple and Jasper rinse the dishes and put them in the dishwasher.

"Do you have a Bible, sweetheart?" she asks Roddie.

"No, ma'am, I don't."

"I have an extra one I will lend you—we will work on getting you one in the meantime." She handed him the Bible, and he smiled as though someone gave him a $50 bill.

"Thanks, Aunt Dimple!" She further tells him that she would give him the page numbers as the Pastor calls out the scripture by the name of the book they'll be reading so that he can follow along.

"I will eventually teach you the books of the Bible—all sixty-six of them," Aunt Dimple tells him.

"Awesome, thanks again, Aunt Dimple!"

"Dude, she's hookin' you up!" Jasper expresses. Roddie is in a zone. Although he doesn't completely know who the Holy Spirit is, he feels the effects of love that the Holy Spirit has allowed him. In the presence of Jasper and Aunt Dimple he feels, comfort, love, and compassion—something he doesn't feel at home. Aunt Dimple instructs the boys to meet her at the car. She takes a moment to make sure the house is secure and sets the alarm. As they arrive at the church, Roddie looks at the church from the rear window in amazement. He feels a little uneasy; remember—it's his first time. Jasper notices that Roddie is hesitant and reserved as they get out of the car.

"Come on, bro, it's okay," Jasper pats him on the shoulder. Roddie just needed a boost of reassurance. The three of them walk to the rear of the church and make their way to the balcony. The inside of the church is breathtaking.

"Roddie, I would like for you to sit between me and Jasper in case you don't understand something." Aunt Dimple suggests. Roddie continues to look around in amazement.

"I'm happy to be here," Roddie expresses. They enjoy service, every bit of two hours; a typical service would last close to one and a half hours. The Pastor is on a roll. His sermon has the entire congregation filled with the Holy Spirit. Roddie takes it all in.

It is time to leave the church, and Roddie is glowing. He doesn't say much as they walk back to the car. Aunt

Dimple and Jasper give him a moment to himself. They both know what he is experiencing…the effects of the Holy Spirit are upon him. "Heck of a rush, huh, bro!" Jasper asks.

"Amazing is all I can say! Wow!" Roddie says. They get in the car and drive off. Roddie sits in the back and looks into the clouds as they continue to drive.

"I can drop you off at home if you'd like, so that you don't have to deal with the bus." Aunt Dimple tells him.

"Sure, Aunt Dimple, I would surely appreciate it." Roddie sits there and continues to look into the Heavens. He doesn't say a word. A few minutes later, they arrive at Roddie's house.

"Hope you enjoyed service. You can go with us anytime."

"Thanks, Aunt Dimple, I truly enjoyed service—I feel something new on the inside of me."

"We understand, bro, thanks for coming. See ya at school tomorrow," Jasper tells him.

"Okay, bro. Thanks for the ride, Aunt Dimple."

"Anytime, Roddie." Roddie gives Jasper a fist bump and closes the door. He slowly walks up the porch. Aunt Dimple and Jasper pull off.

Chapter 9

Fellowshipping

Jasper and Roddie meet at the usual place at school. "Dude, I still feel the rush of the Holy Spirit. So much so that I want to start by following your footsteps and start painting pictures of Jesus for all to see! Besides, aren't we supposed to spread the word of the gospel?" Roddie asks.

Jasper stands still for a moment before he responds. "Dude, you get it! You definitely feel the Holy Spirit—

that's awesome! I was right—I thought I noticed that same glow from yesterday as you were walking this way."

"I can understand how important it is to spread the word. If we can tell others how easy it is to accept Jesus as Lord and Savior, it's the kind of news that we want to spread immediately. I truly believe how important salvation is despite one's past. It's a win-win…confess with your heart and mind that Jesus Christ is our Lord and Savior, and you will be saved…I'm all in!"

"Dude, you are on fire!" Jasper expresses.

"Hey, let's make plans this weekend to start our mission. I want to go downtown and begin there—what cha think?"

Jasper responds: "That's fine with me, but we must paint in an area under a bridge, freeway, or overpass—a place where we don't get caught. To others, it is still considered vandalism although we see it differently. We see it as spreading the word by any means necessary to show those who are lost or those who don't know Jesus at all. I remember Aunt Dimple telling me that God said plant the seed, and He will harvest it."

"Agreed!" Roddie says. They plan to meet at Roddie's house Saturday morning, equipped with backpacks and all that they need to complete the task. They each have a couple bottles of water and snacks to hold them over. It's nine o'clock Saturday morning. They walk to the nearest bus stop and wait on bus number 775 northbound, heading for downtown.

"Ready, bro?" Roddie asks Jasper.

"Ready!" Roddie looks at his watch. "The bus is scheduled to be here in fifteen minutes. I already planned everything out."

"Cool!" Jasper responds. Jasper reaches inside his backpack and takes out a small package of cookies and begins to enjoy them.

"Want some, bro?"

"Nah, I'm good, bro, just trying to watch my figure."

"Really, bro…what figure?" They both laugh. By this time, they notice the bus approaching—it appears to be two blocks away. When it finally arrives, they both grab their backpacks and throw them over their shoulders. Both reach in their pockets and take out a few coins and throw them inside the coin catcher. The bus driver hands them both a small piece of paper that has the date and time printed on them. They head to the back of the bus and put their backpacks in one of two empty seats that are vacant. Of the fifty-four seats that the bus has, only eight of the seats are taken. The entire back of the bus is theirs.

"Okay, bro, it will take us about thirty-five minutes to reach downtown," Roddie tells him.

"Cool, I have time to take a beauty nap," says Jasper.

"A what?" They both laugh.

"I'll wake you up when we get there."

"Thanks, bro," Jasper says. Jasper takes his backpack and places it behind his head and closes his eyes. Roddie takes his phone and attaches the earbuds to it. He places his earbuds in his ear and listens to the music as he enjoys the view. Four songs later, they arrive downtown. He notices that they are three blocks away from their destination. He puts his phone and earbuds inside his backpack and wakes up Jasper as he reaches up to pull the rip cord, notifying the bus driver that they want to get off soon.

"Wake up, bro, we have finally arrived."

"Okay, bro." Jasper wipes his eyes and stretches his arms.

"Man, that was some good sleep. Let's stay on the bus for another thirty minutes, so I can make up for the thirty minutes of sleep that I lost…just joking!" They laugh.

Jasper and Roddie both grab their backpacks and throw them over their shoulders and stand at the exit door. Seconds later the bus comes to a complete stop. Once they get off the bus, they stand there for a couple of minutes to look around and pick a good place to start painting. Jasper gets Roddie's attention and points in one direction.

"How 'bout over there? Looks like the wall is big enough for us both—let's start there."

"Okay, bro, let's go." Roddie approves, and they begin to walk in that direction. The wall is facing a street that has little to no foot traffic. It's the weekend, and most people are spending time with family. The plan is to make sure that people will see the paintings during the weekday—in this case, the Monday that is approaching. Roddie and Jasper approach the wall; they sit their backpacks on the ground. They both kneel and take out several arousal cans and place them on the ground. The cans consist of several colors. Roddie finds a place on the wall that is pleasing to him, and Jasper finds a place on the wall that is satisfying to him. They both begin to paint, looking around from time to time, making sure that the police don't catch them in the act.

Making sure that the coast is clear, they look around in two to three-minute increments. They are fully engaged in the most beautiful artwork that is known to man. Fifteen minutes in, they hear a noise coming from a nearby trash pile. The noise is so obvious that they both look in the direction of the noise. A man has emerged from the pile. He pays them no mind as he takes the debris from around him. The man gets up and walks over to a nearby trash can and digs through it. Jasper and Roddie stop painting for a moment and watch the man as he continues to dig through the trash can. The man pulls out a half-eaten sandwich and begins to eat it. Jasper's eyes light up in disbelief. Roddie reacts to what he sees as well.

"Sir, please don't eat that—that is food that has been discarded by someone who doesn't want it. It is probably old and spoiled and will cause you to become sick," Jasper tells him.

"Yes, he's right—it can make you sick, sir," Roddie tells the man.

The man responds, "I appreciate the concern, but it's all I have."

Jasper bends down and reaches inside his backpack and takes a couple of bags of chips and some crackers, a bottle of water, and hands them to the man. "Here ya go, sir, it's all we have, but you are more than welcome to have them."

Roddie reaches in his backpack as well and give the man a couple of candy bars. "This should hold you over until you get some real food." Roddie reaches into his packet and pulls out a twenty-dollar bill and hands it to the man. Jasper follows suit and pulls out a twenty-dollar bill as well and hands it to the man. The man just stands there, showing gratitude as a tear rolls down his face.

"Thanks, young men, I didn't think anybody cared. It's great to know that God will provide." Roddie and Jasper look at one another.

"Sir, is there any way we can help you?" Jasper asks.

"I'm not asking, but if you want to help me, I will be here most of the time unless it gets cold then I will be at the shelter on the corner of Hope and Fifth street. The city will allow us to take shelter during the winter months."

"Sure thing, sir, we would like to continue to support you if you don't mind."

"That's very gracious. Thanks so much, young men. By the way, what are your names?" the man asks.

"My name is Jasper, and this is Roddie." Jasper reaches out and shakes the man's hand, and Roddie does the same.

"What's your name, sir?" Roddie asks.

"My name is Sam. My friends call me Chester, but Sam will do."

"Okay, Mr. Sam, it's a pleasure meeting you," Jasper continues.

"Likewise, young man. By the way, what are you guys up to? Ya know that painting graffiti is illegal…don't get caught."

Jasper explains what the paintings are and what their intent is about the paintings. "Let me show you something, sir— come a little closer." Jasper takes him to the wall that they are painting and shows him the outline.

"Does something look familiar to you?" Jasper takes his finger and motions the lines that he has drawn thus far.

"Wow!" the man expresses. "It's an outline of our Savior Jesus."

"Exactly!" Jasper responds.

"I'm impressed to see young men so inspired by our Savior—that's not a common thing nowadays. What's the motivation?"

"As the Bible says, we are all to be disciples of Christ and spread the word of the Gospel to the world that they may change their ways and have salvation. Although the Bible doesn't say how, we do what we love to do and paint images of Jesus everywhere we go. Why not do what we love to do and spread the word at the same time? It's a win-win for the Kingdom and for us. Sir, have you seen anywhere in the Bible where is says how to reach out to others and spread the Gospel?"

"I don't recall—I think you guys are correct. I personally don't agree with painting graffiti on the walls; by God, it's justified in this case…amazing!" the man replies.

"With all due respect, sir, we don't paint graffiti—we paint street art."

"I stand corrected." The man chuckles.

"We must continue painting, sir. Are you going to stick around?" Jasper asks.

"Sure, it's not like I have anything to do." Jasper and Roddie grab their backpacks once again and approach the wall. They are truly at work. They take out one can at a time and begin to spray these beautiful colors all over the wall. It amazes the homeless man. Both of them are fully engaged in the paintings as though they are lost in time, continuing to look around from time to time. It takes them forty minutes to finish.

"What beautiful works of art," the man says. Jasper and Roddie have paint all over their fingers. Roddie reaches inside his book bag and takes out a small container. He takes a couple of cotton balls and dips them inside the container and hands a few to Jasper. They begin to wipe the paint from their fingers. The small container has paint thinner in it.

Jasper pauses. "You hear that?"

All is quiet for a moment. They can hear police sirens in the background. The sounds get louder and louder. Roddie and Jasper struggle to put items back into their backpacks.

"Dude, we're in trouble!" Jasper expresses. The sirens are very loud at this point. The police are approaching fast. Suddenly, the sirens begin to fade away. The police are on the next street over, responding to a call several blocks away.

"Okay, Mr. Sam, we have to get going. It was nice meeting you," Jasper tells him.

"Yeah, it was nice meeting you, sir. We'll come see you again, sir—be careful out here." They shake his hand and walk quickly to the bus stop.

"Dude, my heart is still beating out my chest!"

"Mine too!"

"We have to calm down before we bring attention to ourselves," Jasper responds.

"I agree," Roddie expresses. The bus arrives minutes later.

"Dude, that was a bittersweet experience. The fact that we met Mr. Sam was the sweet part—the fact that he lives on the streets is the bitter part," Roddie says.

"Well, the best part is the fact that he knows Jesus and has comfort knowing that Jesus will provide and protect him. We must stick to our word and visit him occasionally," Jasper tells him. They both agree to follow up on their promise.

Chapter 10

CONVICTION

"Bro, please don't be mad at me. I forgot to tell you about the painting contest that is coming soon," Roddie tells Jasper.

"I need more information...what is the competition about, where is the competition, and when is the competition?" Jasper asks.

"Okay, so…I have all of the information. The competition is in a couple of weeks—it's on a Saturday at 1:00 p.m. The entry fee is $40 per person. The competition pays first, second, and third places. First place pays $400, second place pays $250, and third place pays $150—that's not a bad payout, in my opinion," Roddie expresses.

"Put me in, coach. What are the rules and what are we able to paint?" Jasper asks.

"Anything that comes to mind. As you may know, you cannot draw anything that may be offensive. The rules and everything that I just mentioned are located on the website—I'll text it to you."

"Cool, are you joining the competition also?" Jasper asks.

"Sure thing, bro—this is how I figure it. I will win first place and receive the $400, and you will win second place."

"Really, bro?" They laugh.

"Nah, just joking we are not competing against one another—we are entering for the sake of entering a painting contest. This is what we do, bro, and now everyone will be able to see what we do best." Roddie expresses.

"Agreed, bro," Jasper responds.

"I don't recall asking your dad if he has accepted Jesus as his Lord and Savior. Do you remember me asking him? It just dawned on me."

Roddie responds, "Nah, bro, I don't believe you did."

"Well, it's something we must do. No one knows the time of Jesus's return," Jasper expresses.

"Yes, I agree. I remember you explaining how important it is to us all to get into the Kingdom and how easy it is to be saved if we truly believe that Jesus died for our sins and rose on the third day which we call resurrection. I also remember the time that you asked me to repeat after you. This was several weeks ago," Roddie expresses.

"Wow, you remember!"

Roddie takes out his cell phone and calls his dad to see when he would be available for this to take place. Roddie also expresses to his dad why it is so important to meet sooner than later. They all agree to a time and day. Sooner than later, they all meet again. Jasper and Roddie meet him at his usual place, home. Roddie's dad tells Jasper how much he appreciates the fact that he is praying for him again. Jasper is honored to be able to pray and lead him to Christ. Once there, Jasper, Roddie, and his dad are in the front room having a conversation about salvation and how important it is to take heed to what Our Heavenly Father has offered us. Jasper suggests that they begin to pray together.

"Let's all stand." Jasper takes Roddie's hand, and Roddie takes his dad's hand.

"Sir, do you accept Jesus as your Lord and Savior, and do you truly believe that He died for our sins?" Roddie's dad feels the Holy Spirt come into him; he answers.

"Yes, I do!"

Jasper continues to pray as they continue to hold each other's hands firmly.

"I'm proud of you, Dad," Roddie expresses.

His dad turns away, making sure no one sees his emotions. Jasper and Roddie walk outside on the porch and talk.

"That was awesome, bro, thanks for praying for my dad."

"Welcome, bro," Jasper expresses.

Roddie continues, "Hey, I'm feeling some kind of way. Let's promise to go down to the railyard and paint lifelines for the last time. I feel that our Lord doesn't want us to vandalize property. Let's do something in a more constructive way by continuing to paint pictures of positive images that reflect the Bible."

"I feel ya, bro, I've been thinking about that also. Give me ten minutes to grab my backpack and make sure that I have everything I need. Will go to your place so that you can get your backpack also."

"Cool—sounds like a plan," Jasper responds. Roddie goes into the house and grabs everything he needs.

"Okay, Pops, I'm leaving—love ya!"

"Love ya too, son. Make sure and lock up—will talk later."

"Okay, looking forward!" Roddie takes his backpack and throws it over his shoulder, runs into the kitchen, grabs an apple, and makes his way to the front door. When he gets outside on the porch, he notices that Jasper is on his phone.

"Well, bro, I'm all signed up for the competition. You are correct—they said we can paint anything we want as long as it's not offensive."

"Cool, we're both in… Cool! Ready to go?" Roddie asks.

"Ready," Jasper responds. They head for the railyards. It's not the weekend, but they decide to go anyway. The railyard is less active on the weekends, but it's a different story during the weekday—trains are more active. As they scope the railyard, they look for a train that has not been touched; in other words, a train that another tagger has not taken advantage of. As they walk the railyard, Roddie is so eager that he reaches inside his backpack and pulls out a can of paint. He then takes his backpack and throws it back over his shoulder.

"There's one!" He points in the direction of the train that is going about forty miles per hour. He runs toward the train, he readies his aerosol can, and approaches the train. He gets too close to the train. His backpack is caught on a part of the train and rips the backpack from his arm. The backpack is thrown about twenty feet from him. He grabs his shoulder and falls to the ground in agonizing pain.

Jasper yells, "Dude, what the hell!" Jasper makes a mad dash to help Roddie. When he gets to him, he helps him stand to his feet. He takes him over to an old train platform that is not in service and assesses the damage. Roddie is in so much pain that he has tears in his eyes. Jasper runs over to retrieve Roddie's bag and walks back over to him. Jasper takes his backpack and Roddie's backpack and throw's them over his shoulder. He puts his arm under Roddie's armpit and slowly walks him to the street. Jasper is able to get Roddie to a nearby bench and sits him down. Roddie's face is changing colors. Jasper reaches for his cell phone and calls 911; he tells them their exact location. The 911 operator tells him that an ambulance is on the way.

While the ambulance is in route, Roddie squirms as he holds his shoulder. Jasper is not quite sure how much damage is done, but he has no doubt that Roddie has severely injured his shoulder. "Hang in there, buddy!" Jasper says. Roddie barely makes a sound as he continues to hold his shoulder. The ambulance finally arrives fifteen minutes after Jasper calls. Two medics get out of the ambulance and tend to Roddie. One of the medics tells Roddie that it appears that he has ripped his rotator cup. The medic takes some alcohol and a small syringe from a small bag. He takes the alcohol pad and wipes Roddie's shoulder with it. He then takes the syringe and puts it inside a small vial and fills it up. He takes the syringe and slightly pushes the syringe until two squirts come out of the tube.

"Why are you doing that? Doesn't he need every bit of that? It seems like you're wasting it," Jasper expresses.

"I know that you want the best for your buddy, so I will explain to you why it's necessary to do this. I must do this because it takes the air out of the tube before I administer the shot—if not, he will have air in his veins, and that's not what he wants. We appreciate the concerns, young man, but we know what we are doing—trust us," the medic tells him.

"What's that?" Jasper asks.

"It's morphine. Once it gets into his system, he will be very calm. By the way, how did he sustain the injury?" the medic asks.

Jasper is careful about how he responds. He doesn't want to lie, so he tells them that it's a long story and he leaves it at that. "I hope he wasn't doing something he shouldn't," the medic says. Jasper has guilt written all over his face, but doesn't say a word. The medics put Roddie's arm in a sling.

"You're welcome to ride with us as we take him to the hospital."

"Of course, if you allow me to." The medication has kicked in. It's evident because Roddie is knocked out. Jasper calls Aunt Dimple on his cell phone; he tells her what happened and that he would call her back after he calls Roddie's dad. Jasper then takes Roddie's cell phone and calls Roddie's dad. His dad is in shock; he asks Jasper to let him know what hospital they're at once they reach their destination.

Meanwhile, the ambulance arrives at the hospital. They take Roddie to ER. Jasper is with him the entire time until they get to ER. The nurses don't allow him inside. Roddie is taken into surgery. Jasper immediately calls Roddie's dad and gives him the name of the hospital; he then calls Aunt Dimple back. Aunt Dimple tells Jasper that she would come to the hospital to check on Roddie and pick him up.

Roddie's dad makes his way to the hospital. He asks the clerk where his son might be. She tells him that he is in ER and has been taken to surgery. He puts his head down and walks over to the waiting room where he notices Jasper at the vending machine. Jasper tells him everything. Jasper tells him that he and Roddie mean well. Jasper further tells him that this time was the last time they would paint lifelines and concentrate on making a difference by continuing to paint positive images associated with the Bible. He continues to tell him how Roddie was injured. "It was supposed to be the last time we painted in the railyard." Roddie's dad understands and is not upset at either of them.

"I'll stay as long as you'd like, sir."

"No worries. I'll stay here. You can go home and get some rest—after all, you were there when it happened, and you have experienced enough for one day. I'll take it from here. Put my cell number in your phone and lock it in—give me your cell number as well, so I can keep you in the know on Roddie's condition."

"Will do, sir. Thanks," Jasper responds. Aunt Dimple arrives not long after, she meets Roddie's dad for the first time. She is brought up to speed on everything. Jasper and Aunt Dimple leave the hospital. Roddie is released from the hospital four days later. He is in a cast and has a sling to help support his shoulder. He still struggles with his shoulder and takes meds as the pain persists.

Chapter 11

GIVE ME ONE TALON

Jasper visits Roddie at home several days before the competition starts. "Glad you're home, bro." Jasper gives him a brief hug and fist bump. Roddie is receptive and returns with a hug and fist bump.

"Bro! Don't ever do that again! You had me scared to death!" Jasper expresses.

"No worries there, bro, you only saw what happened—I actually felt the pain. Do you think I want to go through this again?"

"Let me help you answer that question…no!"

"Cool! We're good then. You know the competition is this coming Saturday. I want you to know that I am painting on your behalf since you're not able to." Jasper assures him.

"I know, I wouldn't have it any other way! Obviously, I can't paint, so you will represent us both. But I'll be there to support you—I even invited Dad to come." Roddie tells him.

"Gotcha, bro!" Jasper responds. Jasper heads home. He turns in early to get some rest so that he will be prepared for the most anticipated painting contest.

The competition has finally arrived. It's a Saturday afternoon at the local high school where Jasper and Roddie attend. There is a carnival with rides and food vendors outside everywhere. The competition is held inside the school gymnasium. All contestants are present. There are a total of sixteen contestants there from all over the city. Aunt Dimple, Jasper's mom and dad, Roddie, and Roddie's dad are in attendance. Jasper was surprised to see his mom and dad there.

All contestants have custom-made T-shirts with their names on them and badges with their numbers on them, so that the judges can identify the contestants and judge accordingly. The lead judge announces all the rules. The contestants will have covered booths that are assigned to each of them. Once the competition begins, one person (proctor) will be at each booth, holding a small yellow flag to indicate that the artist has completed their work of art before thirty minutes arrives. An air horn will blow once the thirty-minute time has elapsed. Each contestant has several blank canvases to start over at any time during the competition. All contestants would have a total of thirty minutes to finish. All contestants must come out of their designated booths while the proctors bring their covered paintings to the judge's table to be graded.

One by one they call the number of the artist, putting their heads down, grading as the paintings are revealed. There are some very impressive paintings that the artists have painted. Some paintings are of nature, graffiti, and various other displays. The crowd applauds at each painting.

"Number sixteen, you're up!" It's Jasper's time to reveal his masterpiece. The proctor pulls the cloth from his painting. The crowd is amazed at what they see. No one applauds. Seconds pass and Roddie is the first to applaud, followed by Aunt Dimple, Jasper's mom and dad, then Roddie's dad. The remainder of the crowd begins to applaud; the other contestants applaud as well. Jasper painted a beautiful crown with doves in a 3D sort of way, with the words "Redeemer, Comforter, Savior."

"Way to go, bro!" Roddie yells.

Jasper gives a thumbs-up as he looks in their direction. The judges wait until the crowd quiets down. Once they calm down, the lead judge speaks. "All of the judges have tallied all of the possible categories—let's reveal the scores that the judges have."

The judges go from the lowest to the highest possible score that the contestants can have. They start from contestant number 1 and end with Jasper, contestant number 16. The lead judge is handed a small piece of paper to read aloud.

"Third place goes to contestant number 3. The runner-up is contestant number 7, and the winner has been declared number 16."

The crowd goes wild! The lead judge gestures Jasper to approach the judges' table and receive his trophy and hands him an envelope. The lead judge asks Jasper something: "What inspired you to draw such a painting?"

He points in the direction where his supporting cast is standing. "Them!" he states.

The judge looks at him, shakes his hand, and smiles. "Great job!" the judge tells him.

Aunt Dimple invites everyone who is with them to lunch at a fine Chinese food restaurant; she pays for all $145 worth of food and drinks. Roddie and his dad hang out for a while and thank Aunt Dimple for the food; they say their goodbyes and head home.

Meanwhile, the rest of the gang heads over to Aunt Dimple's place to take pictures and chat for a while. Jasper's mom and dad are blown away by Jasper's progress, and they express this to both Aunt Dimple and Jasper. Jasper's parents leave before the sun sets, so that they have enough time to prepare for work the next day. Several weeks pass by, and Roddie improves the motion of his shoulder. He's not 100 percent yet, but he is going to therapy three times a week.

There are three more months of school remaining. Roddie and Jasper have used the remainder of their time to prepare for graduation when they were not painting. Aunt Dimple receives another letter from the courts. It has her address on it, but it also has "the attention of Jasper Smith."

Aunt Dimple calls Jasper on his cell phone to inform him of the letter. "Ahh, man, not again! Can you read it to me, Aunt Dimple?"

Aunt Dimple reads it to him:

> This is Judge Rose Simpson. We have just recently found out that you could potentially be responsible for painting images of the Bible all over the city. No need to be alarmed because crime has gone down expeditiously. If you are responsible, we would like for you to please show up at the courthouse sometime this week. Showing up will

confirm that you are the person or persons responsible. An admission of guilt, if you will. It will take a lot of taxpayers' money to clean up the drawings. If you are responsible, I will not prosecute you. We prefer that you paint in an art studio or gallery of some sort and not on city structures. I have talked this over with the courts, and we have agreed to give you a grant to open your own studio and teach others to paint as well. This offer is valid once you finish high school, of course. Call the county clerk at the phone number below to make an appointment. Looking forward to seeing you.

Sincerely,
Honorable Judge Rose Simpson.

"Aunt Dimple, if another letter comes from the courts, please throw it in the trash."

"Well, why would I do that?" she asks.

"Well, every time a letter comes my heart beats so fast that I don't believe I will recover from it!"

Aunt Dimple laughs. "God is good—He has given you favor. A second chance, a talon if you will. Look at the Revelation—that is wonderful, young man. This is what happens when you are obedient. Spreading the Gospel is what you and Roddie are doing."

"Yes, ma'am. God is awesome!"

Jasper immediately calls Roddie. "Are you busy? I have something to tell you. I just received a letter from the county. The same judge that I had to face in court sent me a letter!"

"Dude! What did she say?" Roddie asks.

"Hold on to your seat." Jasper explains the letter and what it says in detail. As Roddie takes it all in, his eyes grow the size of hard-boiled eggs.

"Dude, we are finished!" Roddie expresses.

"Calm down, bro, remember she has offered a grant, so it's not all bad."

"Sorry, bro, you're right. I was just focused on these words that were rapidly running through my mind: judge, courts, caught, hand cuffs, police, jail, et cetera."

Jasper laughs aloud. "Huh, I had similar thoughts also. The judge asked me to make an appointment to see her later this week. I want you to go with me."

"Say, bro, no strings attached, right?"

Jasper responds, "Like I said, bro, relax…no strings attached." Jasper gives him reassurance. Roddie eventually calms down and agrees to go to the county courts with Jasper. Jasper tells Aunt Dimple that Roddie is going to the courthouse with him.

"By the way, I would love for you and Roddie to get baptized together. I can call the pastor to make arrangements—I strongly suggest this. Call Roddie and let him know what I just shared with you and see if he is available any Sunday. I will wait to call the pastor until we know for sure when he's available," Aunt Dimple says.

"Now that sounds like a grand idea, Aunt Dimple. I will call him back ASAP." Roddie gets home, and his cell phone rings not long after he gets comfortable; he notices that Jasper is calling, so he answers his phone.

"Sup, bro, what cha doin'?" Jasper asks.

"I'm just sitting here with the remote in one hand, watching TV, and the other one propped up on a pillow. Dude, the stuff they show on TV is crazy—what is this world coming to, an end?" Roddie expresses.

"That 'bout sums it up. Let me share something with you. God's wrath will come down hard on people if they don't take heed to his word and turn from their wicked ways. There are prophecies being fulfilled every day around the world. Earthquakes, floods, wars, famine, droughts, and other things that let us know that the end is approaching fast. God gives us a free moral choice. My mom told me about the movie *Noah's Ark* she used to watch when she was a teenage girl. The story was about a man named Noah and his family. God spoke directly to Noah and told him to build an Ark which is a huge vessel. God told Noah to take all animal species of all kinds—male and female—so that civilization could start over again. God was preparing for a great flood to cleanse the earth of wicked people. These people were given the opportunity to repent and change their lives. Most of them did what they wanted to do. They continued to party, warship idols, drink, have sex, and other things that God has disapproved of. To add insult to injury, the people mocked Noah, made fun of him, and called him crazy. Noah was obedient to God and finished the Ark. The people continued to disobey. The rain began, but the people thought that the rain would stop, so they continued to party and worship idols. After several days, the people realized that it had not stopped raining and the water was rising. The water had risen so high that there was nowhere for people to go."

"So what happened to the people?" Roddie asks.

"The people drowned."

"What!" Roddie expresses.

"That was the point I was making—God sends us messages by fulfilling prophecies to get our attention. It seems that Noah's Ark is repeating itself in history. We all are to be disciples and spread the word of the Gospel to others—that is the very reason we do this with our street art."

"Deep, bro, deep," Roddie says.

"This is the reason I initially called you," Jasper tells him.

"Sup, bro?" Roddie responds.

Jasper continues, "Listen, I was talking to Aunt Dimple, and she suggested that we both get baptized together. What is your feeling on the subject?"

"Well, I know that I haven't been living up to my standard, so I am slow to answer that question."

Jasper interrupts him, "Let me break it down this way. The Lord knows who we are. He also knows that day by day is a challenge for us to keep and uphold his commandments. In the Old Testament, it states that we had to sacrifice an animal every time we sinned. God knew that mankind could not keep these commandments—it was too difficult. So He arranged it so that we can live by grace and grace alone, which is sufficient for believers that have faith."

"Will you explain what grace means?" Roddie asks.

"Sure, I'll try to explain as best I can. Grace is something we don't earn or do. It is God's provision that he gives us to offset sin. In other words, it's a promise, covenant between us and Him. That simply means that he forgives us for our shortcomings and doesn't condemn us. He gives us the ability to think before we act, to have a conscience so-ta-speak."

"Sorta like a get out of jail free card," says Roddie.

"That's correct!" Jasper expresses.

"Once again, you've explained it as though you've been spending time in the Bible," Roddie says.

"That's because I have, bro," Jasper expresses. "Should I take that as a yes?" Jasper asks.

"Yes, take that as a yes—I'm all in!" Roddie expresses.

"Speaking of reading the Bible, why don't we read together say next week for at least half an hour—you down?" Roddie asks.

"Sure thing, we can do that. Cool, I'll call Aunt Dimple so she can schedule this with the Pastor. What Sunday is good for you?"

"This Sunday would be great if we're able to." Jasper reaches out to Aunt Dimple, and she, in turn, reaches out to the pastor. The pastor has baptism on first and third Sundays, and the next Baptism would be third Sunday since the first Sunday has passed. This would put them two weeks out. Aunt Dimple tells Jasper that the date is all set for third Sunday. Jasper relays the message to Roddie as well.

"Since you young men decided to get baptized, I want to show you how much I appreciate you both—I would like to buy you both a suit. It's the least I can do—you guys have matured in Christ, and I'm proud of you both. Call Roddie and tell him that I would like to take you both to the mall this coming Friday. I want you both to be well-dressed for the baptism. I might even throw in lunch!"

"Awesome, Aunt Dimple. Thanks so much!" Jasper expresses.

"Have you ever worn a suit?" Aunt Dimple asks.

"No, ma'am, I haven't."

"When you talk to Roddie, ask him the same question, if you will."

"Sure, Aunt Dimple, I'll call him back and ask him." Jasper calls Roddie to let him know what Aunt Dimple said regarding the baptism. He also asks him if he has ever worn a suit before.

"Bro, I'm honored. Let me put it like this—this will be the first time I will try on a suit, look at a suit, and God forbid own one—well, yeah! Going to the mall and having some fresh clothes to wear for our special event. This is a very special occasion indeed," Roddie says.

"Aunt Dimple is buying lunch as well—bro, that's a win-win as far as I'm concerned."

"Aunt Dimple is one of a kind!" says Roddie.

"Great! I will let her know. I'm excited as well!" says Jasper.

The date is set; they all agree on the upcoming Friday. Life goes on. Jasper and Roddie both anticipate owning their own suits. The day has arrived: Aunt Dimple allows Jasper to drive to pick up Roddie. Roddie can drive as well, but his license has a couple of speeding tickets that he has to pay for before he can legally drive again. Jasper pulls up in front of Roddie's house. Jasper blows the horn twice to let Roddie know that they are outside (Roddie's dad is at work). Roddie runs to the door and peeks out of the window and notices that they have arrived to pick him up. Roddie locks the door and runs toward the car. He jumps in the back seat and hugs Aunt Dimple from behind. He gives Jasper a firm fist bump.

"Aunt Dimple, do you really trust him to drive?" They all laugh.

"Aunt Dimple, I can't express how much I appreciate what you are doing for us. I have not had this kind of love expressed in a while," Roddie tells her.

"You are very welcome, sweetheart!" They have a small talk before they arrive at the mall. When they arrive at the mall, they visit several stores. Roddie is the first one up to be fitted. As they check his inseam, arm length, waist, and neck sizes, he just stands there with his eyes closed and arms spread wide as though he's a celebrity with a net worth of $50 million. Jasper and Aunt Dimple just sit back and laugh. They are enjoying each other to the fullest.

Chapter 12

We Can See Clearly Now

Roddie and Jasper pick out some nice suits to wear. The store clerk takes each suit and places them inside a plastic covering to protect them. The clerk and his assistant take the suits to the register. The clerk asks if they needed anything else. "Now, what would a nice suit need to complete this order? Well, how about a couple of ties to go with the suits?" says Aunt Dimple.

"Sure, ma'am," the clerk responds. "The ties are over there in that section." The clerk points toward the section where the men's ties are located.

"I will hold the suits behind the counter as you pick out the ones you want."

"Thanks—let's go get some ties, fellas," Aunt Dimple responds. All three walk over to the tie section. Jasper and Roddie look at several ties that they can choose from. Jasper finds a tie that he likes, and Roddie has three in his hand to choose from.

"Dude, you can only choose one tie," says Jasper.

"I'm having a hard time trying to decide which one matches my suit—I'll be back." Jasper shakes his head while Aunt Dimple stands there patiently. Roddie takes the three ties and heads back to the counter; he asks the clerk for his suit and places all three ties down beside the suit.

"I like that one. I'll put these back," Roddie says.

"No worries—I put them back," the store clerk says. Roddie gestures for Jasper and Aunt Dimple to come back to the counter.

"Ready," Roddie says. Jasper shakes his head once more. The clerk takes both suits from behind the counter and places them on top of the counter and scans the items. Aunt Dimple reaches inside her purse and pulls out her wallet that had her credit card in it. The clerk gives her the total amount that's due, and she hands the clerk the card.

"Almost forgot—we need to ask the clerk to demonstrate how we tie the ties—I've never owned one, so I wouldn't know how," says Aunt Dimple, and they all laugh.

"My dad knows how—he used to wear them all the time. He'll have no problem showing me and Jasper. Speaking of Dad, I don't believe he's been baptized either—I will ask. If he hasn't, is it okay if he joins me and Jasper?"

"I don't see why not. The more the merrier—that's how our Heavenly Father sees it. Let me know as soon as you are able."

"Will do, Aunt Dimple," Roddie tells her.

"You fellas ready to eat?" Aunt Dimple asks. They leave the mall and go to one of Aunt Dimple's favorite restaurants. They go to a Super Buffet. When they walk inside, Jasper and Roddie light up like fireflies. They have never seen this much food on display at one time.

"Dude, it's on!" Roddie expresses.

"You don't have to tell me twice—let's go!"

"Ring me up for three adults—reluctantly my perception of these two says otherwise," she tells the cashier. Aunt Dimple and the cashier just laugh. Aunt Dimple gets her receipt and picks out a booth. She walks over to Jasper and Roddie and points in the direction of the booth. She then walks over and takes a clean plate and walks over to the buffet. Roddie and Jasper follow her. Once they've filled their plates, they all sit down. One of the employees asks each of them what they want to drink. The employee goes to a nearby drink station, makes the drinks, and brings them back to the table.

"I want to apologize, Aunt Dimple, I was hungry," Jasper says.

"Me too, Aunt Dimple, I'm sorry," Roddie says.

"No worries, guys, I totally understand—I am hungry as well." They hang out for a while and enjoy their meal. Roddie's dad calls him back later. He tells Roddie that he has not been baptized. He also tells him that he would love to get baptized on the same Sunday. Once Aunt Dimple finds out that Roddie's dad wants to partake in the baptism, she is filled with joy. She calls the pastor and sets everything up.

Several days later, Roddie and Jasper go down to the courthouse and met with Judge Simpson. Jasper introduces Roddie to the Judge. While Roddie is in front of the judge, he is a man of very few words. "Young man, you are the kind of person most would conclude to be interesting. This is a bittersweet moment for me. I like what you are doing and the purpose behind it, but painting on city structures is a no-no, and I have to enforce the law and put citizens that paint graffiti on our buildings in jail. But there is an alternative. That is why we are here."

"Sorry, ma'am, we call it street art," Jasper explains.

"I understand, young man. I will explain the terms of the grant to you." She read the terms aloud. "I will print you a copy, so that you can have an adult look it over. Make sure to bring it back and leave it with the county clerk. We will have the grant put into a trust on your behalf. You have the talent and influence to change lives. Off the record, I am also a believer in Christ, and that's one of the reasons why I support you and encourage you. To be so young and anointed, you have embraced revelation early on. I am proud of you, young man."

"Thank you, ma'am. I can't take all of the credit—my sidekick Roddie has a lot to do with the paintings as well," Jasper explains.

"Wow! The Lord has anointed you both—a bundle package, if you will. I wish the both of you well. I will show up one day to the art studio to see the progress of your manifestation," the judge expresses. Judge Simpson reaches out her hand and shakes both Jasper and Roddie's hands. Jasper takes the envelope and secures it, making sure he doesn't lose it.

"You can breathe now, bro," Jasper tells Roddie.

"Hey, can you call your dad and see if he can show us how to tie our ties?"

"That's a great idea," Roddie responds. Roddie calls his dad. His dad gives them the okay to come through. They leave the courthouse and head over to Roddie's house. They spread the great news of the grant to everyone. Once Jasper gets home, he hands it to Aunt Dimple. Aunt Dimple examines the grant and its terms and later gives it to her sister to read (Jasper's mom).

Sunday morning, the day of the baptism: Jasper is in his room, preparing for the big day. Aunt Dimple is in the kitchen, finishing up breakfast. "Breakfast is ready, young man!" she informs Jasper.

"Yes, ma'am, I'm coming!" Jasper makes his way to the kitchen. Meanwhile, Roddie and his dad are preparing as well. His dad makes chicken and waffles for them both.

"It's been a while since I cooked breakfast. Don't get me wrong—this is a very special occasion for the both of us. I am very proud of you. What I wanted and expected from you has been fulfilled—I have the Lord to thank for that," his dad tells him.

"Dad, I'm glad you've come around. It has been difficult to talk to you up until now—thanks for listening to me. This gives me peace." Roddie and his dad embrace each other.

Aunt Dimple asks Jasper to call Roddie to make sure they all met in a central location at the church at a designated time. Roddie tells Jasper that him and his dad will meet them in the church parking lot. They all agree to meet a half an hour before service starts at the south entrance of the church. Church service starts at 10:00 a.m. this Sunday. The four of them meet at 9:30 a.m. as planned. When Roddie and Jasper get out of the cars, heads turn in their direction. Aunt Dimple is looking sharp, wearing her favorite dress and hat to match. Surprisingly, Roddie's dad is wearing a new suit as well. He didn't want to be left out, so he discreetly bought a suit of his own. He looks like a million bucks. Aunt Dimple brought her digital camera and asks one of the members to take a picture of them.

Jasper, Roddie, and his dad had previously received a welcoming letter from the church, instructing them what to bring to the baptism. The three of them are carrying a small bag of swim shorts and a towel. Before service starts, they are all given a locker to put their items inside. When the pastor instructs them, all the candidates will follow the ushers to the baptism pool. One side is for the woman and the other for the men. On this Sunday, there are four other people that will be baptized as well. Aunt Dimple, Jasper, Roddie, and his dad sit together in service.

Twenty minutes after the praise team sings a couple of songs and gets the congregation going in the Spirit-filled sanctuary, the pastor calls for all the baptism candidates to head to the baptism pool. All candidates go into their respective places separated by gender. Pastor has on his white robe and a small towel laying across his right shoulder. He baptizes the ladies first one by one. The pastor gestures the women to walk down three steps and into the pool. He instructs them to cross their arms across their chest and relax. The pastor makes a statement before each candidate is baptized: "You will go down dirty with past sins and will come out clean with repentance."

After the women are baptized, the congregation goes crazy. The men are up next. Like the women, the pastor gestures each man one by one to approach the baptism pool. Roddie and his dad are not far in front of Jasper— one, two, and three in that order. Pastor asks each candidate if they have truly accepted Jesus as Lord and Savior. Once they nod their heads, he submerges them in the pool. Aunt Dimple is in front with her digital camera, snapping several pictures of the three of them as they are all emotional. It was surely a Kodak moment.

Three weeks later, Jasper sits in his classroom, taking notes as the teacher lectures. He gets an unexpected call from his mom. "Hey, sweetheart, are you sitting down?"

"Hello, Mom, let me go into the hallway." He gets permission from his teacher and walks out to the hallway.

"I'm surprised that you are calling—this is unusual. Why did you ask if I'm sitting down, Mom?"

"We just got a call from the ER. Aunt Dimple was admitted to the hospital by ambulance, and she was pronounced DOA," she explains.

"What is DOA, Mom!"

"It means dead on arrival. As ambulances transport patients, they try to revive them, and if they don't respond and have no pulse, then they have passed away."

Jasper drops his phone and screams as loud as his vocal cords allow. His teacher and more than half the class empty into the hallway. His teacher picks up his cell phone and continues to talk to his mom. His mom is emotional and can barely get a word out. It takes Jasper a while to get himself together. He is taken to the nurse's office to be treated for a migraine headache. His mom tells the teacher that she is on her way to the school. Jasper's mom shows up thirty minutes later and goes to the nurse's office. Jasper is lying on a small cot with a towel on his head.

When his mom walks in, Jasper gets up and grabs her, holding her tight. Jasper's mom asks the nurse if her and Jasper could have a private moment together. "That's not a problem. I'm the nurse, but you're the mom, and you can give him more care than I can at this moment. I'll be in the next room over," the nurse expresses.

The nurse grants her request and leaves the office. "I'm in extreme pain as well. My emotions are all over the place, so I understand, sweetheart. Sit down—I want to share some things with you, and there is no better time than now. You and I know that Aunt Dimple loves you very much—no question there. Aunt Dimple had an illness that only me and your dad knew about. Despite her illness, she took you in. You were too young for us to disclose this to you. We felt that we needed to protect you and your emotions. If me and your dad had taken this lightly, you could have turned into a criminal, or worse, committed suicide. We didn't want to roll the dice with your life. Besides, we fell on hard times, so it was best to ask Aunt Dimple if she could be your guardian. Me and your father both also knew that she was shaping and molding you to be a strong man in Christ, and we unselfishly allowed the Holy Spirit to do what the Holy Spirit does best. We let the Holy Spirit take its course. When things started looking up for us, we wanted to bring you back home, but you had grown so fond of Aunt Dimple that we decided to let you stay with her until you graduate from high school. Aunt Dimple was fond of you as well. She would always call you a 'nonproblem child.' She was pleased that you had dedicated your life to Our Heavenly Father. Her intention was to mold you to be the young man that you have become. She has dedicated these few years of her life to better yours. She kept me and your dad up to speed on your progress and maturity. That's how we found out about the competition and the grant, amongst other things—we were very informed. She told me about you going to court. She told me that she only revealed this to me because I kept pressing her—otherwise, she would have never told me your little secret. Ever since we were little girls, your Aunt Dimple has always had a major and positive impact on people's lives, with her big heart and compassionate ways. She, too, had an anointing on her life early on. Since me and Aunt Dimple were the only two siblings, she left me and your dad the house, and she left you a small box, her Bible, and the car."

Jasper lights up. "Wow!"

"There is only one condition to having the car—she wants you to continue to drive it to church."

"That's not a condition—that's an honor, Mom!" Jasper expresses. He looks up. "Thanks, Aunt Dimple, for everything!" he expresses.

He and his mom are emotional once again. He maintains his composure once more. "I have to call Roddie, Mom!" His mom hands him his cell phone. He speed-dials Roddie. Jasper is trying to hold his emotions as Roddie answers the phone. "Sup, dude?"

"We lost Aunt Dimple!" Jasper expresses.

"What! What did you say, dude!" Roddie sets the phone down, and you could hear him crying loudly in the background. He doesn't return to the phone. Jasper hangs up the phone and gives Roddie a moment and calls him back later. Roddie eventually tells his dad. The entire family is beside themselves. Pastor makes funeral arrangements not long after the baptism; he never would have thought that one of his most dedicated members has passed away at such a time. Jasper's mom pulls out a letter and reads it to him. It's from Aunt Dimple to the attention of Jasper.

> Mission accomplished: my intention was to shape and mold you as a strong man in Christ. All along I was sick with cancer and the Lord brought you into my life at the right time. Make no mistake, our God is sovereign. He can and will do as he pleases. Although he has the power to control our will, He gives us free will to do as we please, be it right or wrong. However, the decisions that we make in life will either make us or break us. In other words, if you have the will to do right, He will reward you, and likewise, if you have the will to do wrong, there will be consciences that you will face. The consequences can and will be severe. The Holy Spirit will always be with you to help you make

the right decisions, but this is only if you take heed to his instruction, be obedient and faithful. I've noticed that your friend Roddie is also on the same path. I want to encourage you both to sharpen each other for the Kingdom's sake. Continue to uplift one another during the adversity that you are going to face. Our Heavenly Father says that we will be like sheep among wolves. Stay planted like the roots of a tree. Our Heavenly Father will always be with you; don't forget. Reach as many people as you possibly can because prophecy is being fulfilled. Reach out to those who are lost and don't know God, and those who have fallen—get them back on their feet. It is your God-given talents that He has anointed you with. He has given you a talon; don't bury it. Continue to sow your God-given talon and watch

> manifestation take place. Plant the seed, and our Heavenly Father will harvest it.
> I will see you again, my love…
>
> Aunt Dimple.

Jasper and Roddie graduate from high school. They receive the grant from the city and open JR's art studio. Mr. Sam is no longer on the streets; he is an employee of JR's art studio and school. He oversees all the facilities, maintenance, grounds, and anything that is needed to keep the facilities maintained. They also start a foundation for cancer in honor of Aunt Dimple. Yes, Judge Simpson visits the studio with some of her colleagues and they purchase several paintings among them. Roddie's dad joins the church and is now an usher. Eventually, Jasper and Roddie open several stores throughout the county. They hire several employees and are able to open an art school and teach full-time. They have both encountered manifestation, and both receive a very hefty salary. The two of them sow back into the Kingdom.

About the Author

Author Anthony S was born and raised in Los Angeles, California. First and foremost, he would like to acknowledge our Heavenly Father for sustaining him and giving him the vision to write two different genres. He writes urban fiction with a message behind each book he writes. He also writes children's books. Meet his character Paradise. He not only entertains children but he also educates them, teaching morals.

Get to know him as an author as he is eager to build his fan base. Visit him at www.booksbyanthonyS.com and tccomnow84@gmail.com to contact him for signings and updates. Blessings! Thank you for supporting him…